P.J. CLOVER · PRIVATE EYE
The Case of the Missing Mouse

For Kathy —
Best wishes —

Susan Meyers

Other P.J. Clover, Private Eye Books

P.J. CLOVER · PRIVATE EYE
The Case of the Missing Mouse

by Susan Meyers

illustrated by Gioia Fiammenghi

Fawcett Columbine • New York

A Fawcett Columbine Book
Published by Ballantine Books
Copyright © 1985 by Susan Meyers
Illustrations copyright © 1985 by Gioia Fiammenghi

Library of Congress Catalog Card Number: 89-91599

ISBN: 0-449-90459-8

This edition published by arrangement with E. P. Dutton
(Lodestar Books), a division of NAL Penguin, Inc.

Cover design by Bill Geller
Cover illustration by Joel Iskowitz

Manufactured in the United States of America

First Ballantine Books Edition: March 1990

10 9 8 7 6 5 4 3 2 1

to Sid Fleischman,
for saying the right thing
at the right time

Contents

I

Too Much Business

Something was up.

I was sure of it.

Otherwise, it didn't make sense.

P.J. Clover and I had been in business—the private eye business, that is—for only one week, and already we were swamped. Already we were drowning. Already we were up to our necks . . . up to our ears . . . up to the very tippy tops of our heads in business.

Too much business.

That was the problem.

"I don't get it," I said. I put my eye to the peephole we'd drilled through the center of the eye on our clubhouse door and peeked out at the crowd gathered in P.J.'s backyard.

It was a Thursday afternoon, and there were kids all over the place. Buddy Robertson from down the block, Cynthia Davis, Mike Pratt, Gigi Gumpers, and lots more whose names I didn't know. All of them were little—in the first or second grade—and all of them were giggling and shoving and whispering as

1

if they had some big secret that no one else knew.

"I just don't get it," I repeated, stepping back from the peephole before the kids could notice and start clamoring for me to open the door. "Where are they coming from?"

P.J. Clover (the initials are short for Pamela Jean, but don't ever call her that . . . not if you value your life!) looked up from the blue, red, and yellow pushpins, each one representing the scene of a crime, that she was sticking into a map of Mill Creek which hung on the clubhouse wall. Her straggly blond hair was sticking out every which way. There was an ink smudge on her nose and another on the Mickey Mouse T-shirt that she was wearing.

She was a mess, to put it bluntly. But she didn't care.

P.J. Clover is *not* a girl who cares how she looks.

P.J. Clover is a girl with *bigger* things on her mind.

"They heard about us," she said, cheerfully stabbing another pin into the map. "They heard about the absolutely brilliant way I—I mean, we—solved our first case."

P.J., as you can see, is not exactly modest!

"Good news travels fast, you know!"

"But not *that* fast," I said.

I, as you can see, am a worrier. And being P.J. Clover's best friend and partner gives me plenty to worry about!

Like this private eye business.

It was supposed to be fun, of course. At least as much fun as the fortune-telling business or the dog-walking service or the bug museum that P.J.—who's always full of big ideas—had cooked up in the past.

2

In fact, when she'd found the sign that looked like an eye and hung it on our clubhouse door, painting her name and the word *private* above it and my name, Stacy Jones, and the word *associate* below it, I'd been more excited than ever before. I'd always wanted to be a detective, a daring private investigator like Nancy Drew or one of those guys you see on TV. I'd even been the one who thought of drilling the peephole right through the center of the eye.

But I'd never expected anything like this. Why, the paint P.J. had used to write our names on the door was barely dry. How could those kids camped out in the backyard have found out about us so fast? How could a sleepy little town like Mill Creek, California—population: 15,000; location: just outside San Francisco—suddenly become so full of crime?

"It just doesn't make sense," I said. "Why, it's almost as if they're up to something. Trying to wear us out. Trying to put us out of business, even! I mean, look at these, P.J."

I pointed to the pile of file folders filled with the details of cases stacked on the rickety old card table we used as a desk.

"Why, there's enough crime here to keep the Mill Creek police force busy for years!"

"But that's just the point," said P.J. "*We're* not the Mill Creek police force!"

She turned away from the map to grab a pickle and peanut butter sandwich (one of her favorite combinations) from a plate on the table. She took a bite. It seemed to give her renewed energy.

"Don't you see?" she said, starting to pace back and forth.

She couldn't go very far because our clubhouse—which is made from an old toolshed we got from Mr. Sabatini down the block—was packed to the rafters with shelves, boxes, cabinets, and crates. All things that P.J. had scavenged to hold the files full of information she expected to gather in the pursuit of crime!

"These are the kind of cases the police don't have time for," she said. "Lost dolls. Missing baseball mitts. Stuff that's not important to grown-ups, but that really matters to kids." Her eyes sparkled with enthusiasm. "It just goes to show that Mill Creek needs us. It just goes to show that stupid old Butch Bigelow is wrong!"

So that was it!

I might have known she'd be thinking about Butch.*

"He says we don't belong in the private eye business," she said, biting a big piece out of her sandwich and swallowing it down in one gulp. "Says we were

---

*I won't have any other footnotes, I promise. But Mrs. Crane, my creative writing teacher (fifth grade, Park School) says they're a good way to get in additional information. And I have to tell you somewhere about Butch. Because he's going to be important—*very* important—to this story.

Anyway, Butch Bigelow is P.J. Clover's nemesis, her enemy, her rival. I don't know exactly why—though it may have something to do with them both liking to be the center of attention—but ever since nursery-school days they've been fighting. Back then it was about who could hold his or her breath the longest and who could eat the most paste. Now it was about . . .

But wait. Go back to where you were. I'll let P.J. tell you herself!

4

just lucky, solving our first case the way we did."

(That's the case—in case you haven't read it—of the stolen laundry. P.J. bet Butch that we'd solve it in record time, and we did. Naturally, Butch didn't like that. He'd been trying to get back at P.J. ever since. And from the way she was carrying on now, I'd say he was succeeding.)

"Says we'll never be able to do it again," she fumed. "Well, I'll—I mean, *we'll* show him. We'll solve all these cases in no time at all. And then smart alecky Butch Bigelow will have to shut up for good!"

"But P.J.," I began.

I was going to say that she'd been trying to get Butch Bigelow to shut up for years. I was going to say that it would take more than solving a few cases to make him stop. I was going to say that Butch wasn't worth bothering about anyway. But I didn't get a chance. Because just then the crowd outside started acting up.

"Hey, come on," someone yelled, pounding on the clubhouse door. I thought I heard Gigi Gumpers giggle.

"Yeah," a chorus of voices followed, sounding almost rehearsed. "We've got crimes here. We need this stuff solved."

Again, I heard Gigi's giggle. And again, I was sure I was right. "P.J., something strange is going on," I said. "Those kids are up to something. I don't know what, but—"

But before I could finish my sentence, before I could do anything—such as fasten the lock or escape out the window—the door was shoved open.

A small boy was pushed through.

5

And *that*—though I didn't know it at the time—was the beginning. The beginning of our second big case!

The boy was little. He couldn't have been more than four or five years old. And he was nervous. He peered anxiously around the inside of the clubhouse. "I . . . I'm supposed to see the . . . the eye," he whispered.

P.J.—who I don't think had been paying attention to any of my comments—stepped forward proudly. "At your service," she said.

She snapped her fingers in my direction. "Stacy, a clean file," she ordered.

I gritted my teeth as she turned back to the boy. "Now tell us," she said grandly, "what is your problem?"

The boy looked relieved.

(I guess he'd been expecting to see a real eye floating from the ceiling or something!)

He also seemed confused. "My, uh— Oh, my problem," he said. He scratched his head. "Just a minute," he muttered as he reached into the pocket of his overalls and pulled out a wrinkled piece of paper.

"What's that?" asked P.J.

"My case," the boy replied. "It says what I lost. He wrote it, only . . . only I can't read."

He held the paper out to P.J.

"Is it OK?" he asked nervously. "Do you pay me now? Or do I have to get the money from him?"

"Money? Pay you?" P.J.'s eyebrows shot up in surprise as a hand reached through the half-open door of the clubhouse and grabbed the boy by the straps of his overalls.

"Dummy!" I heard Buddy Robertson hiss as he dragged him out. "You weren't supposed to show her that. Now you've spoiled it. Now he probably won't pay any of us."

P.J., frowning suspiciously, looked at the paper the boy had given her.

I could see that it was covered with big messy writing. And as P.J. read it, her face suddenly turned scarlet.

Her hand, the hand holding the paper, began to shake.

And then a strange gurgling, strangling sort of sound escaped from her throat.

She reminded me of a volcano about to erupt. And in a second, that's exactly what she did!

"The worm!" she exploded.

She whirled around to stare at the map of Mill Creek, at the pushpins that dotted it like rainbow-colored measles. "All these cases," she moaned. "Wild-goose chases."

For a moment she looked as if she were going to cry. But in a flash, she recovered herself.

"Well, he's not going to get away with it!" she exclaimed, grabbing me by the arm and pulling me out the door. "He'll wish he'd never thought of such a sneaky, low-down scheme. He'll wish he'd never heard of P.J. Clover, private eye!"

2

The Scene of the Crime

We were halfway across the yard, on the way to Butch Bigelow's house, before I realized what was going on.

P.J. didn't explain, of course. She was too angry.

But she did hand me the paper the boy had given her. And when I recognized Butch's handwriting (*Tell her your cowboy hat was stolen from* . . . the message began) and when I remembered what the boy had said about getting paid and what P.J. had said about wild-goose chases, I suddenly knew that I'd been right! Something *was* going on. Something awful, terrible, but brilliant. Something more brilliant than I ever would have expected Butch Bigelow to think up.

I'll explain it quickly, in case you haven't figured it out already. What had happened was this:

Butch Bigelow had made up a bunch of phony cases. He'd hired little kids who didn't know any better to bring them to us. It was just as I'd thought. There wasn't any crime wave in Mill Creek. There was just Butch, trying to drive us out of our minds. Or, at least, out of business!

"The worm!" P.J. exclaimed again.

And this time, I agreed. Butch Bigelow might be jealous of P.J. (for all I knew he might still be angry at her for eating more paste!) but he didn't have any right to ruin the best idea she'd ever had.

The kids outside our clubhouse were mad, too. Because although Butch had hired them, he hadn't yet paid them. When they found out we were onto his scheme, they figured they'd better come along.

"'Cause *we* did what we were supposed to," one of them said, trying to look innocent. "We deserve to be paid."

"You bet you do," P.J. agreed. "And I'm going to see that you are paid. Plenty!"

I don't know what she had in mind.

Butch's life savings, perhaps? Or maybe his scalp!

But there was no time to find out. We were already rounding the corner to Butch's block. I was working so hard trying to keep up with P.J., whose legs are nearly twice as long as mine, that I didn't even notice what was going on at the other end of the block.

I didn't notice until Gigi Gumpers suddenly stopped giggling.

"Hey, look!" someone shouted. "The police!"

I heard P.J. draw in her breath.

I looked up.

I saw a black-and-white patrol car pull to a stop in front of a red house with white shutters. Two officers leaped out and dashed up the path. Right straight up the path to Butch Bigelow's house!

Someone—it looked like Butch—opened the door and the policemen disappeared inside.

"Maybe there's been a robbery," one of the kids piped up.

"Or a murder!" another one exclaimed.

That was all P.J. Clover needed. "Come on," she said, starting to run. "They may need help!"

It took me a moment to get my legs moving. My heart was suddenly pounding. The word *murder* echoed in my ears. In other words, I was *scared!*

By the time I reached Butch's house, P.J. was already bounding up the steps. The front door was open.

Without a moment's hesitation, P.J. dashed inside.

I felt weak in the knees, but I had to follow. Taking a deep breath and wishing my heart would stop hammering, I stepped into the Bigelows' living room.

No one was there.

(No bodies on the floor either!)

But excited voices were coming from down the hall.

"You mean you called us all the way out here for a piggy bank?" a deep voice was saying.

"Not a pig, a mouse."

"Butch," a woman's voice sighed. "How could you?"

"Well, it was stolen!" the voice that I recognized as Butch's came again. He didn't sound confident, the way he usually does, though. He sounded, well, desperate.

"It had . . . it had my . . . my money in it," he stammered.

I looked at P.J. I could see that she thought Butch sounded strange, too.

"Come on," she whispered, grabbing me by the arm and pulling me down the hall in the direction of the voices. "We've got to find out what's going on." Her nose gave an excited twitch. "This *could* be exactly what we need!"

11

I wasn't sure what she meant, and there was no time to find out. We'd already reached Butch's room and stopped in the shadows just outside the door.

Butch's mother was standing in the middle of the room apologizing to the police. She had her coat on, her handbag slung over her shoulder, and a sack of groceries in her arms. "If only I'd known he was calling you," she was saying, "I would have stopped him. But I was out. I got home just a moment before you arrived and—"

"But Mom," Butch protested. He hadn't noticed P.J. and me. "My bank's gone!"

"Yes, but—"

"I've *got* to get it back!"

"But Butch, it couldn't have had much in it," Mrs. Bigelow said. "I don't see why . . ."

Butch opened his mouth as if to say something. His face beneath his mop of curly brown hair was pale and worried. His freckles stood out like miniature chocolate drops.

P.J. and I exchanged a glance. It was clear we were thinking the same thing. This wasn't the smart-alecky Butch Bigelow *we* knew, the sneaky low-down Butch Bigelow who'd been trying to put us out of business.

Something—something much more important than just a piggy bank being missing—must have happened. Something that had him scared. Something that he didn't want his mom to know about.

"I . . . I need it, that's all," he finally said.

The taller of the two policemen sighed. "All right, let's not argue," he said. He took a notepad and pencil from his pocket. "We're here, so you may as well tell us what happened. From the beginning."

Butch gave the officer a grateful look. He *still*

hadn't noticed P.J. and me. "Well, it was right here," he said, pointing to a junk-cluttered desk in front of a window. "It was here this morning when I left for school. Then, when I came home after doing my paper route, it . . . it was gone!"

"How about that door going from your room to the backyard? Was it locked or unlocked?"

Now *that* was a good question.

But it didn't come from the policemen, who should have asked it. No. It came from P.J. Clover!

Butch whirled around at the sound of her voice. "What are *you* doing here?" he said as she stepped into the room.

"We came with some friends of yours," P.J. replied. There was a wicked gleam in her eye. "We thought you might need help. Though, of course, we're pretty busy right now."

Butch gulped. He knew what friends she meant. He knew what we were busy with.

I saw him shoot a nervous glance at his mother.

"Well, I've got help," he said quickly.

At that, the policeman with the notebook roused himself. He must have finally realized that *he* should have asked that question about the door. Or maybe he was just embarrassed at being shown up by a skinny, straggly-haired girl in a Mickey Mouse T-shirt!

Anyway, holding his pencil ready, he inquired in an official-sounding voice, "Just how much was in this bank?"

The question made Butch gulp again. "Well, it wasn't exactly . . . I mean . . ."

"How much?" the officer repeated.

"Six dollars and thirty-three cents," Butch replied, his cheeks turning an embarrassed shade of red.

"Six dollars and . . ." The policeman exchanged a glance with his partner, who rolled his eyes toward the ceiling.

Then he jotted the figure down and snapped his notebook shut. "Right," he said. "Well, I think that's all the information we'll need." He nodded to Butch's mother.

"I'm terribly sorry about this," she said.

"All in the line of duty," the police officer replied.

"But my bank. My . . . my money," Butch sputtered as the policemen turned to go.

"We'll keep an eye out for it," the officer who'd rolled his eyes toward the ceiling said kindly, but firmly. "We'll do what we can. Meanwhile, I'd do some checking myself if I were you. Since your bank seems to be the only thing in the house that's missing, it could be that one of your friends is playing a joke. That happens, you know."

He looked suspiciously at P.J. and me.

I felt my cheeks get hot. Was he suggesting that *we'd* taken Butch's old bank? And how could he call it a joke? Six dollars and thirty-three cents might not be much to a grown-up, but it's a lot to a kid!

P.J. must have been thinking the same thing. But unlike me, P.J. Clover doesn't just think. She acts!

She pulled a small white card from her pocket and thrust it at the policeman. "I beg your pardon," she said. "But this young man is *not* our friend."

She paused dramatically.

"He is our client!"

15

3

A *Real* Case

Butch's mouth dropped open.

The policeman didn't look quite so astonished, but he *was* at a momentary loss for words. He glanced at the card.

It was one of our business cards, of course. A newspaper reporter had them made for us when we solved our first case. This is how they look:

P.J. CLOVER • PRIVATE

NO CASE TOO LARGE
NO CASE TOO SMALL

Stacy Jones, associate
phone 388–9456

The same reporter also wrote a story about us in the paper which, apparently, the policeman had read.

"Ah, I've heard about *you*," he said, a look of recognition coming into his eyes. He passed the card to the police officer who had been taking notes and added with a grin, "It's the Lone Ranger and Tonto."

"The what?" I heard myself exclaim. I don't lose my temper often, but when I do . . .

Well, if P.J. hadn't stopped me, I might have been in big trouble. Because assaulting a police officer is a crime!

As it was, the other officer stepped in quickly to calm things down.

"Maybe these girls will be able to help," he said soothingly. His voice sounded serious, but I thought I noticed the hint of a wink aimed in his partner's direction. "I've heard about them, too," he went on. "Just about everyone down at the station has. You're a pretty lucky fellow," he said to Butch—who looked as if he might throw up right then and there!—"having P.J. Clover on your side."

Well now!

That certainly made up for the Lone Ranger and Tonto bit. Though I think he might have mentioned me, Stacy Jones, associate, while he was at it.

P.J. took it as if it were her due. "We do our best," she said humbly as Butch collapsed onto the bed.

The officer looked satisfied. He turned to Mrs. Bigelow. "Be sure to call us if it turns out anything else is missing," he said.

"Oh, I will," Butch's mother replied, following the policemen out of the room. "And I'm so sorry about all this. He's a very well-adjusted boy, you know. But he has such an *active* imagination. . . ."

A long, low groan escaped from Butch's throat as

the footsteps died away down the hall. And I couldn't help feeling just a bit sorry for him. After all, no one wants to be described as "well-adjusted."

P.J., however, wasn't wasting any time on sympathy. *She* was ready for work. "Have you got your notebook?" she said to me.

She didn't need to ask. A writer *always* has her notebook handy. I pulled it from my pocket, and though I still couldn't believe what was happening, I flipped to a clean page, took a pencil from my other pocket, and wrote:

Date: Thursday, Sept. 26

Time: 5:15 p.m.

Crime: ~~Piggy~~ Mouse bank stolen

Client: Butch Bigelow !!

Butch, meanwhile, was coming out of his trance. He stared at me, scribbling away in my book.

He blinked as if *he* couldn't believe what was happening either. "Hey!" he exclaimed. "What's going on? What do you think you're doing?"

"Getting started," P.J. replied.

"Getting started?" Butch leaped to his feet. "What do you mean, getting started? Getting started on what?"

He stood in front of P.J., his hands on his hips, his chin thrust out like a bulldog's.

The effect was spoiled, of course, by the fact that he couldn't look her in the eye. He had to look up, because P.J.'s taller. She could have patted him on the head. But she didn't. She's not *that* foolhardy!

Instead, she replied calmly, "On your case, of course."

"On my case!" Butch's curly hair practically stood on end. "Oh, no, you're not!"

"Oh, yes we are," P.J. said. "You owe us one, Butch."

Butch's face turned red again. "I don't know what you mean," he muttered.

Suddenly, I got mad. "Yes, you do," I said, remembering all those phony cases I'd written up, all those pushpins I'd stuck in the map, all that worrying I'd done. "You owe us a case, Butch Bigelow. A *real* case!"

He squirmed. I could see he realized his innocent act wasn't going to work. I could also see he was worried. After all, he was the victim of a crime, a crime that no one was taking seriously except P.J. and me.

"Well, what makes you think you can solve it?" he asked half belligerently, half hopefully. "The police couldn't."

"The police wouldn't," P.J. corrected. "That's why Mill Creek needs us. That's why you need us. And that's why I, P.J. Clover, am prepared to make you a deal!"

"P.J.," I warned.

I was going to say "Be careful." Because P.J. Clover's deals have gotten us into plenty of trouble in the past. But I could see she wasn't listening. I could see she was thinking. I could see she had something big up her sleeve.

"We'll take your case," she said, "and if we don't solve it, we'll hang up our hats. We'll go out of business. We'll—"

"P.J.!" I exclaimed. "We can't do that."

"Why not?" she said. "If we can't find a simple little thing like a piggy bank . . . ?"

"A mouse," Butch interrupted. "It wasn't a pig, it was a mouse."

"Pig, mouse, what difference does it make?" P.J. said impatiently. "If we can't find it, we don't belong in this business. But if we *do* find it"—she turned to Butch—"if we do," she said, "then *you*"—she poked her finger into Butch's chest—"you have to swear a solemn oath."

Butch stepped back. "What kind of an oath?" he said suspiciously.

"An oath never—and I mean never, ever—to bother us again."

I could see by the shocked expression on Butch's face that he thought it was an inhuman request.

But I thought it was brilliant. And I was ashamed of myself for ever doubting P.J. Because if we could get Butch Bigelow to stop bugging us just by finding a little old piggy, I mean, mouse bank, then it would be the best deal P.J. Clover ever made.

"Well?" said P.J.

Butch hung back.

"You're going to need that money," she warned, nodding toward the window. There, gathered in

Butch's backyard, were the kids who'd followed us from our clubhouse. The kids he'd hired and not yet paid. They looked mad. I guess they'd found out there hadn't been a murder, and now they were thinking murderous thoughts of their own!

"Where's our money?" they called when they saw Butch peep through the glass.

Though the window wasn't open, their voices came through loud and clear.

"I'm going to tell my father on you," Cynthia Davis threatened.

Butch gulped. Cynthia's father was the butcher at Mill Creek Meats. He had arms as big as hams.

"I'm going to tell your mother," Gigi Gumpers yelled.

That did it. "All right," Butch said quickly. "All right. It's a deal."

"A wise decision," P.J. declared, rubbing her hands together in satisfaction. "And now"—she looked Butch straight in the eye—"now, suppose you tell us what was *really* in that bank!"

Butch took a step back. "What do you mean? I mean, how . . . how do you know . . .?" he stammered.

"Because you wouldn't call the police for six dollars and thirty-three cents," P.J. interrupted. "You just said that because your mother was here. There's something you don't want her to know. Something . . ."

At that, Butch glanced nervously toward the door. "Don't talk so loud," he whispered.

We could hear his mother still apologizing to the police in the living room.

"Then tell us," P.J. insisted. "Tell us what was really in that bank."

It was a struggle. I could see it on Butch's face. But

finally he managed to get out a word. "Three . . ." he began in a squeaky sort of whisper.

P.J. leaned forward eagerly. "Go on," she urged. "Three what?"

"Three hundred . . ." Butch almost choked on the words.

My mouth dropped open.

I saw P.J.'s eyes open wide.

"Oh, what's the use," he groaned. "I might as well say it. I might as well tell you the truth. It was three hundred. Three hundred and six dollars and thirty-three cents!"

4

Mickey Mouse

For a moment, even P.J. was too astonished to speak. She stared, dumbfounded, at Butch. Finally, she murmured, "It must have been an awfully big pig."

"Mouse," Butch corrected. "I keep telling you, it wasn't a pig. It was a mouse. A mouse like on your shirt."

P.J. looked down at her T-shirt. She has so many that I guess she forgot which one she was wearing. "You mean Mickey?" she said. "It was a Mickey Mouse bank?"

"Yeah," Butch replied. "But it wasn't babyish," he added quickly, "because it was old. Real old. My grandmother gave it to me. It belonged to my grandfather and . . ."

"But how did you get that much money?" I interrupted. I thought all this chitchat about his grandfather had gone on long enough. "How did you fit it into a little piggy, I mean, mouse bank?"

Butch grimaced. "Easy," he replied. "I just dropped it in. All in one piece."

Now I was really confused. But P.J. (whose mind sometimes works quicker than mine) seemed to catch on right away.

"All in one piece," she repeated. Her nose gave an excited twitch. "You mean— Butch, doesn't your dad have a coin collection?"

Butch, looking more miserable than ever, nodded.

And suddenly, I saw what P.J. was getting at. Mr. Bigelow *did* collect coins. He'd brought some to school to show us. He'd had a penny that was worth a hundred dollars. A dime that was worth more than two hundred . . .

"It was a nickel," Butch said. "A 1937 buffalo nickel. But the buffalo had only three legs. They made a mistake when they minted it. That's why it was worth so much."

"But what was it doing in your bank?" I said, still not quite able to believe what I was hearing. "Why wasn't it with the rest of your dad's collection? Or in a safe or somewhere?"

I could see by the expression on Butch's face that that was something he didn't want to think about, let alone talk about. But he'd started, so he had to go on.

"I was looking at it, that's all," he replied. "It was yesterday afternoon. My dad's out of town until Saturday, and I just wanted to have a look. I had the money from my bank spread out on my desk because I thought that maybe some of my nickels . . ."

His voice trailed off. Obviously, none of *his* nickels had had buffaloes with only three legs!

"Anyway," he went on quickly, "some of the guys came by and—"

"Guys?" P.J.'s ears perked up at that. She nudged me in the side to remind me of my notebook. "What guys?"

Butch bristled. "Hey, wait a minute," he said. "None of my friends are thieves."

"No, no, of course not," P.J. agreed quickly. Though I don't think she meant it. "We just have to get all the facts."

"Well . . ." Butch didn't look convinced, but I guess he figured since he was in so far, he might as well go on. "Well, there was just Jason Miller, Mike Keegan, Adam Berkowitz," he said as I scribbled down the names.

"And a couple of younger kids, too—Kevin Fisher, Willy Jones. They were getting up a soccer game. They wanted me to go to the park with them."

"And did they see the nickel?" P.J. asked. She couldn't keep her nose from giving another excited twitch.

"No," Butch replied. "They saw the money, I guess, but not the nickel, because I just scooped it all up— my six dollars and thirty-three cents and my dad's nickel—and dropped it in the bank. You see, they were in a hurry, so I figured I'd just put the nickel in the bank and get it out later. But then I forgot and . . ."

"And now the bank's gone," P.J. said.

"And your father's coming home Saturday," I said.

I could certainly see why Butch looked so miserable.

I glanced at P.J. I thought I detected a flicker of sympathy in her eyes. After all, you'd have to be pretty hard-hearted (which P.J. Clover is not) to feel anything but sorry for someone in poor Butch's shoes.

Before she could say a word, though, Mrs. Bigelow suddenly came back into the room. She looked mad. Mad with a capital *M*.

"What am I going to do with you, Butch?" she demanded, speaking to him as if P.J. and I weren't even there. "I have never been so embarrassed in my life. I've been out there apologizing my head off to those police officers. Hearing about how much it costs to come out on a false alarm."

"But it wasn't a false alarm," Butch protested. "My bank and Dad's—" He stopped himself just in time. "I mean, my bank is gone!"

"Did you look for it?" his mother said, not noticing the slip he'd almost made. "It's probably around this room somewhere. You probably forgot where you put it. I don't see how you can find anything in this rat's nest anyway!"

She *did* have a point. The room was not exactly tidy. But I didn't think she should be talking like that in front of P.J. and me.

"Mrs. Bigelow," I said, as politely as I could manage, "do you really think Butch would forget where he put his *money*?"

That stopped her. She was still angry. But she saw my point. "Well, no," she admitted. "I guess not. A bank's not quite the same as dirty socks, is it?"

She managed to smile slightly, and some of the tension went out of the air.

"But I don't see what else could have happened to it. If it's not misplaced, then it was stolen. Or at least, taken. But who—"

"That's what we're trying to find out," P.J. interrupted. She flicked a strand of straggly blond hair out of her eyes and tugged her T-shirt into place. "Now for starters," she said. "Suppose you tell us exactly who was in this house today."

Butch's mother looked surprised.

(I guess she'd forgotten that P.J. and I were private eyes!)

But now, as she looked P.J. over—taking in the straggly hair, the smudge on her nose, the Mickey Mouse shirt—she seemed pleased. She murmured something about a more appropriate level of response (whatever that means) and smiled a genuine smile.

"All right," she agreed. "If you think it will help. But I'm afraid it was a pretty busy day around here."

And *that* turned out to be the understatement of the year. Because by the time she'd finished, my hand was practically falling off from writing so much so fast. I was wondering how *I'd* gotten the job of taking notes in this business. And I was thinking that a better question might have been, "Who was *not* in this house today?"

Anyway, here's the list just as Mrs. Bigelow gave it to us (the underlinings and comments are mine, of course):

Who was in the Bigelows' house
the day of the crime:

1. Man from gas company —
checking heater in Butch's room

2. Mr. McMurphy — new principal
of Park School (that's our school).
Came to see Mrs. B because
she's president of P.T.A.

3. Mrs. Bigelow's Brownie troop: 10
girls. (But I'm not going to write
all their names.)

4. Monica Fisher (ugh!) helps
Mrs. B with the Brownies

5. Fuller Brush man

6. Avon Lady

7. Myra Jones, Mrs. Bigelow's
neighbor — to borrow an egg
(sounds suspicious!)

Well, you see what I mean. Long. And tiring. In fact, I was surprised Mrs. Bigelow was still on her feet after a day like that.

"Did anyone besides the man from the gas company go into Butch's room?" P.J. asked.

Butch's mother frowned. "No, of course not. That is . . . well . . ." She hesitated. "Well, I guess I don't really know," she admitted. "You see this is my day off from work, and I was trying to do some cooking and baking for the week. I had to keep going into the kitchen to keep an eye on the stove and— But this is ridiculous. None of those people would have taken Butch's bank! Not my neighbor Myra. Not the Brownies. Not Monica Fisher!"

She looked expectantly at P.J. But P.J. said nothing. She was probably thinking of the first rule of a private eye. The one she'd made up herself. The one that went *Trust no one . . . suspect everyone!*

"I wouldn't put it past Monica," Butch grumbled.

At that, Mrs. Bigelow looked genuinely shocked. "Why Butch, you should be ashamed of yourself," she said. "Monica Fisher's an angel. You could learn a few things from her."

The disgusted look on Butch's face showed what he thought about *that.*

I knew how he felt. Monica's not really such a bad sort, but she works so hard at being good that most of the kids at school can't stand her. Her younger brother, Kevin, is the exact opposite. He's always in some kind of trouble. In fact, I think that maybe Monica tries to be good just to make up for him!

"Such a dedicated girl," Mrs. Bigelow went on, ignoring the look on Butch's face. "Rushing here after school to help with the Brownies even though she had so much homework she had to leave early. Why she's—"

But fortunately, we didn't have to hear any more about angelic Monica Fisher, because just then an alarming noise came from the kitchen. It sounded like a pot bubbling over.

"My soup!" Mrs. Bigelow cried, and without another word about Monica or Butch or his bank she dashed from the room.

Butch and I exchanged a glance. "I guess she wouldn't really do it," he said. And I agreed.

Monica can be a pain—always chosen to take notes to the principal's office, handing in typewritten reports, winning spelling bees—but she isn't a thief.

"No, I suppose not," said P.J., with a touch of disappointment in her voice. "But someone else *is*! We'll have to check everyone on that list. And we'll have to check this room for clues." She began to sort through the stuff on Butch's desk. It was a motley assortment —half-finished model cars, Lego toys, dominoes, a box of hamster food, dirty socks, a pile of *Star Wars* comics.

"Nothing much here," she announced after a moment, picking up an old banana peel and dropping it back on the heap. "Just a lot of junk."

"Junk!" Butch exclaimed.

I don't think he liked hearing his treasured possessions described as junk. And I'm sure he didn't like having his room inspected for clues by P.J. Clover!

P.J., of course, paid no attention to his objections. She left the desk and opened the door leading from Butch's room to the backyard. "No good," she announced. "Cement. No footprints. But there may be fingerprints." She quickly removed her hand from the

31

doorknob. "We'll have to come back with our finger-printing kit."

"Our *what*?" The words were out of my mouth before I could think. "P.J., we don't have—"

P.J. shot me a withering glance, and I shut my mouth quickly.

"Of course, we'll have to take measurements," she went on, dropping to her hands and knees, and beginning to crawl over the carpet as though she were a bloodhound. "Find out how far it is from the door to the— Aha!"

She stopped, her nose almost level with the rug.

"What is it?" Butch demanded, dropping to his knees as P.J. picked something up from the carpet. "Show me! It's *my* room!"

P.J. held out her hand. In her palm lay a small, metal disk. As I leaned closer, I saw that it had a picture painted or, perhaps, enameled on it. A picture of none other than Mickey Mouse!

"It's not mine," Butch said, before P.J. could even ask. "I never saw it before."

"You didn't?"

P.J.'s nose gave a twitch. And I knew she was thinking something important.

"You did say your bank belonged to your grandfather?" she asked Butch.

"Yeah, but—"

"And the money. I don't mean just the nickel, but any money. Could you get it out easily?"

"Yeah," Butch replied, looking puzzled. "The bottom of the bank screws off. But what's that got to do with . . . ?"

"Just checking," P.J. spoke quickly. Her eyes were

33

sparkling. I could tell she was trying to hide her excitement. "Just checking," she repeated. She slipped the disk into her pocket and stood up before Butch could say another word.

"Come on," she whispered to me. "We've got work to do!"

"But . . ." Butch struggled to his feet. "Where are you going? What are you going to do?"

By this time, P.J. had regained her composure. She paused, one foot in the hallway, the other in Butch's room. Then she gave him her most dazzling smile.

"Why, we're going to solve your case, dear boy," she said grandly, sounding like an actress on one of those English TV shows my mother's always watching. "So don't you worry about a thing. . . ."

She swept out of the room before Butch could make a move.

"Remember, you're a pretty lucky fellow . . . having P.J. Clover on your side!"

5

The Trail of the Missing Mouse

Butch's bellow of rage followed us all the way
through the living room and out the front door.

The kids who'd been part of Butch's dirty trick
were hanging around on the sidewalk now.

"What's going on?" Gigi Gumpers demanded.

"Are we going to get paid?" Mike Pratt asked.

P.J. waved them aside.

"Don't worry," she said airily. "My client will pay
you. Soon. Now run along home."

I thought she was laying the English duchess stuff
on a bit thick. P.J. does get carried away sometimes.

How could she be so sure we'd get Butch's bank and
the three-legged buffalo back so soon? What did we
have to go on? Just a list of names—some of them, like
the man from the gas company and the Avon lady, not
even names. We had no real clues except that little
button or whatever it was.

"Do you think it's important?" I asked.

The kids, grumbling to themselves, were taking
P.J.'s advice and heading for home.

"That little button, I mean." By this time we were halfway down the block with P.J. in the lead, of course.

"Could be," she replied, without stopping.

"Then why in the world did you want Butch to think it wasn't important?" I said.

This time she did stop.

"Because we don't want him to solve his own case, that's why," she said, looking at me as if I were slightly dim-witted. "*We've* got to solve it!"

"But do you think we can find it?" I said, starting to worry again. "I mean, you don't know who took it. Or do you?"

"Not exactly," P.J. replied slowly. "But I think I may know *why*. This little whatever-it-is"—she pulled the metal disk from her pocket and held it up in the rapidly disappearing afternoon light—"this little fellow . . ." She wiggled the button so that Mickey seemed to be dancing a jig. "This gives me an idea!"

And that was all she would say.

She had to think, she told me as we reached my house and she left me at the end of the walk.

"But—" I began.

"No buts," P.J. interrupted. "And no backing down."

(As if I would!)

"We're on the trail," she said, lowering her voice and looking around suspiciously as though the trees had ears. "The trail of the missing mouse!"

Missing mouse? Missing money was more like it.

Still, I couldn't help glancing over my shoulder as she spoke. Maybe the trees *did* have ears. Maybe the thief was hiding in the hollyhocks. Or maybe . . .

Well, anyway. You see the kind of mood P.J. Clover can create!

There was no getting anything more out of her, though. She was gone, down the block to her house, before I could say a word.

There was no chance to talk on the way to school the next morning either because I had to go early. I had to help my mother cart a whole bunch of stuff into the auditorium for Parent Night, which was being held that evening.

By this time, I was pretty annoyed. Annoyed at P.J., that is.

I mean, here we were in business together, and she wouldn't tell me what she was doing. Or, at any rate, thinking.

I was also worried.

Because I'd thought of something. Namely, that the police were right. No *grown-up* would steal a kid's piggy—or rather, mouse—bank when there were valuable things like watches and radios and jewelry lying around.

No one but Butch could have known about the three-legged buffalo inside the bank, and that meant that whoever took Butch's bank had to be a kid. Now, there were only three kinds of kids on the list in my notebook.

Monica Fisher, who we'd already eliminated.

Butch's friends, who Butch had eliminated.

And the Brownies.

My heart sank at the thought. A Brownie, a thief! "Stacy, be careful!"

My mother took the bunch of dried leaves I was holding—or I should say, squeezing—and stuck them

37

into a vase. "Very pretty," she pronounced. "I'm not going to set up the rest of the decorations yet, though. I want them to be a surprise for Mr. McMurphy."

I was thinking so hard about the Brownies that it took me a minute to figure out who Mr. McMurphy was. Then I remembered. He was the new principal of Park School. He was taking over because our regular principal, Mrs. Elwood, got sick.

I'd written his name on the list in my notebook because he'd visited Mrs. Bigelow yesterday. He'd visited my mother too, because she's vice-president of the P.T.A. She'd been raving about him all through dinner last night. "Such an interesting man. Such an interesting hobby . . ."

But at that point, my brother, Victor, and I had gotten into a fight about who was going to clear the table, and I'd never found out what the principal's hobby was. Now I couldn't have cared less.

Hardly paying attention to what I was doing, I helped my mother carry a few more boxes from the car into the auditorium. She was still talking about the new principal.

"You haven't seen his office yet," she said. "No, of course you haven't," she answered herself. "You haven't even seen him, have you? But I understand he has his whole office full—"

But before she could finish, the first bell rang.

I set the punch bowl I was carrying down on the table and, leaving my mother to fuss with the dried leaves, went looking for P.J.

She wasn't hard to find. All I had to look for was the crowd. It was gathered in the schoolyard just outside our classroom. And P.J., of course, was right in the center.

She was wearing her Mickey Mouse T-shirt, the same one she'd worn yesterday, and she was talking—some might have called it bragging—about how *she*, or rather, *we* (as she quickly put it when she saw me) were going to find Butch Bigelow's bank.

She didn't mention the nickel. Fortunately. And Butch wasn't there. More fortunately still.

But Monica was. She was standing at the edge of the crowd, and one look at the expression on her face told me *she* was worried, too. Suddenly, I realized that she might have the same suspicions I had. She might think a Brownie had taken the bank, too.

"P.J.," I said, pushing my way through the crowd. "Wait."

But P.J. didn't.

"Justice," she declared nobly, lifting her chin a notch. "Justice will be done!"

Monica turned a shade paler. She opened her mouth as if to say something. But then the tardy bell rang. The crowd broke up, and Monica—who, of course, is never tardy—hurried into the school building with the rest of the class.

Finally, P.J. paid attention to me.

"Where have you been?" she exclaimed, not bothering about the tardy bell that was still sounding. She grabbed me by the arm and pulled me inside the building. We ducked into the little alcove by the drinking fountain. "We've got a lead!" she said.

As she spoke, she pulled something that looked like a newspaper clipping from her pocket.

But I didn't wait. If I've learned one thing, it's that with P.J. you've got to speak up fast. And this was important.

"Listen, P.J.," I said, "I don't think this is an ordinary crime."

"You bet it's not!" P.J. agreed.

"I mean, it's not a matter of justice being done and all that," I went on. "It's more like a . . . like a mistake."

"A mistake!" P.J. echoed.

"Well, sort of," I said lamely. Of course, I knew that stealing was never a mistake. But if one of the Brownies had taken the bank, we should at least give her a chance to explain. P.J. didn't seem to be catching on, though.

"Look," I began again, "Mrs. Bigelow will know how to handle it. She could begin by giving them a little talk . . . on honesty."

"Honesty?" P.J. repeated. "Them? Who do you mean, them?"

"Them," I said, glancing nervously toward the classroom where everyone was already seated.

I'd never known P.J. to be so dense!

"*Them*. The Brownies."

"The Brownies!" P.J. exclaimed. "You mean you think . . . ?"

"Well, who else?" I said, dropping my voice to a whisper. "But maybe whichever one did it couldn't help it. She wouldn't have known about the nickel, and maybe the money was just too tempting. Six dollars and thirty-three cents is—"

"Six dollars and thirty-three cents!" P.J. looked at me as if I'd lost my mind. "Stacy, you've got it all wrong!" she hissed. "We're not talking about six dollars and thirty-three cents. We're not even talking about a buffalo nickel!"

41

She waved the newspaper clipping she'd pulled from her pocket in my face.

"We're talking about something bigger. Much bigger."

She paused. "We're talking about a mouse," she said, lowering her voice to an excited whisper. "A mouse that *could* be worth a fortune!"

For a moment I didn't know what to say.

A mouse worth a fortune?

Inside our classroom, I could see Monica Fisher and the rest of the class sitting attentively at their desks. I could hear Mr. Collins, our teacher, taking roll. He was on the *B*'s. There was still time, if we hurried, to slip into our seats. If we were quiet and if Mr. Collins kept his eyes on the roll book, we might make it without getting caught.

But I had to find out what P.J. meant.

"Read this," she said, shoving the newspaper clipping at me. "It's from Sunday's paper. I thought I remembered seeing it."

I took the clipping from her.

The headline leaped out at me: MILLION-DOLLAR MOUSE! it said.

"Read it," P.J. urged, glancing up and down the hall. "Before someone finds us out here."

I didn't have time to do a really careful job of reading it. I was nervous, and every sound in the hall made me stop. But what I did manage to see was enough to make me catch my breath.

The article wasn't quite complete because P.J. had torn it from the first page of the Home section without getting the rest of it—the part that was continued on

42

page 33. ("My mother used that to wrap the garbage in," she explained.) But what she did have was enough. More than enough.

It was all about Mickey Mouse stuff—old stuff like Butch's bank that had belonged to his grandfather—becoming valuable. It said that one old Mickey Mouse comic had sold for $200. And old Mickey Mouse watches had gone for $2000!

"See what I mean?" asked P.J. excitedly. "And look at the last paragraph."

My eyes traveled to the paragraph headed Collectors To Meet This Saturday.

Quickly, I took in the words. A convention of Mickey Mouse collectors was being held in San Francisco on Saturday. There'd be lots of buying, selling, and trading. It would be the biggest market for Mickey Mouse memorabilia—that's what the article called it—in the country.

"You see?" said P.J., grabbing the paper back from me. "There's the motive. That's why someone would steal Butch's bank. They're going to take it to that convention and sell it for hundreds, maybe even thousands, of dollars!"

It was hard to believe. A kid's bank, a *treasure*? No, more than that. I was forgetting the three-legged buffalo. A treasure within a treasure!

"I started to suspect it when I found that little metal disk with the picture of Mickey on Butch's rug," P.J. said, whispering quickly. "I figured it came unglued from a cuff link or a pin. Maybe even a tie clip. And who would wear something like that? A Mickey Mouse collector, that's who. It could have been any of those people in Butch's house yesterday. Or even someone who saw the bank through the window. The back door was unlocked. They could have walked right in.

"What really proves it," she went on, "is that the whole bank was taken. That's why I asked Butch if it was easy to get the money out. Remember? Because if it was easy, and if all the thief wanted was money, then he would have just unscrewed the bottom. He wouldn't have taken the whole bank."

She was right, of course! And suddenly, I started to worry all over again. Because looking for a plain old piggy—or rather, mouse—bank taken by a Brownie was one thing. But this . . . this was beginning to sound dangerous.

"What do we do?" I asked. "Go to the police?"

"We may have to," P.J. replied, which showed how serious she thought it was. "But first, we're going to the library. They have catalogs there of things people collect. We've got to make sure we're on the right track."

I could tell she was thinking about that Lone Ranger and Tonto remark. P.J. Clover was *not* about to be laughed at again.

"We'll look up Mickey Mouse stuff," she went on, "and see if we can find a bank like Butch's. Then we'll . . ."

But before she could say what we would do next, there was a shuffling of books and papers in the classroom. I turned around quickly. Mr. Collins had finished taking roll. Class was beginning.

"Uh oh, now we're in for it," I groaned.

I was trying to figure out a way to slip into the classroom unnoticed, when Monica Fisher appeared at the door.

44

She had the attendance sheet, the attendance sheet without our names checked off, in her hand. There was no hope now. In a moment Monica would do her duty. In a moment she would sound the alarm. In a moment . . .

But I was wrong.

Instead of marching right back into the classroom and telling Mr. Collins where we were, Monica held a finger to her lips. She glanced furtively up and down the hall. "Sh," she whispered, drawing closer to P.J. and me.

I looked at P.J. She was looking at Monica.

And I could tell we were both thinking the same thing.

Monica looked the same as always—tidy sweater, neat pleated skirt, wavy hair held back by a barrette —but she certainly wasn't acting the same.

She grabbed P.J. by the arm. "Quick," she whispered, as P.J. stared at her in astonishment. "You've still got time. You can still sneak in. He's writing on the blackboard. He won't see you and I'll . . . I'll just . . ." She seemed to choke on the words. "I'll just check your names off the list."

"You'll do what!" I said.

But Monica paid no attention to me.

She was looking at P.J. Squeezing her arm—desperately.

"Only please," she said. "Please don't try to find Butch Bigelow's bank!"

6

The Third Request

You've heard the expression "You could have knocked me over with a feather"? Well, that's how I felt. Until I remembered the Brownies.

"Wait a second, Monica," I said. I remembered how worried she'd looked in the hall. I remembered how worried I'd felt. "We don't suspect *them*. We don't suspect the Brownies. Not anymore."

Monica looked startled.

For a moment, I could have sworn she didn't know what I was talking about.

Then, "You . . . you don't?" she whispered. She looked nervously from P.J. to me and then back to P.J. again. "Then . . . then who . . . ?"

But before either of us could reply, the door across the hall, the door to the principal's office, suddenly opened. A man with brown hair, blue eyes, and a droopy mustache stepped out. I knew right away that it must be Mr. McMurphy, the new principal. But what a way to meet—tardy and talking in the hall!

He looked at the three of us crowded into the alcove by the drinking fountain. "What's this?" he said, frowning.

Monica looked as if she were about to faint. She lowered her eyes. She seemed afraid to look at Mr. McMurphy.

I felt sorry for her. If this wasn't the kind of first impression *I* wanted to make on the new principal, imagine how *she* must feel!

P.J. must have felt a twinge of sympathy, too, because she stepped forward quickly.

"Sorry for the disturbance," she said before Monica could give way completely. "But we had some business to discuss. *Important* business."

Mr. McMurphy frowned again. He looked P.J. over, taking in her straggly blond hair, her freckled face, her long skinny arms and legs. Then his eyes came to rest on Mickey, smiling jauntily from her T-shirt, and his frown turned into a smile.

"Well, I don't know what's going on here," he said. "But at least you're a . . ."

Before he could say what P.J. was, though, Mr. Collins came out of our classroom. "What's going on out here?" he asked.

"Important business, I gather," Mr. McMurphy answered. There was a twinkle in his eye now. "But not more important than class, I hope."

"Oh, but it is," said P.J. eagerly. "It's . . ."

I held my breath, hoping she wouldn't decide to reach into her pocket, pull out one of our cards, and present it to the principal with her usual flourish.

Fortunately, she didn't have a chance.

Mr. Collins had taken charge.

"That's enough, P.J.," he said. "Monica, take that

47

attendance sheet to the office. I'm sorry about this," he added, turning to the principal.

Monica, with a final worried glance at P.J., hurried away down the hall.

"It's not usually so noisy around here." Mr. Collins explained. "At least not this early in the morning."

He began herding P.J. and me toward the classroom.

Mr. McMurphy said something about not minding a bit of noise and turned to go back into his office.

Out of the corner of my eye, I saw the door open. There was a brightly colored poster on the wall. Reds, yellows, blacks. But the door closed before the picture could register in my mind.

Not that I *cared* what the new principal had on his office wall. I had too many other things to think of. Things like million-dollar mice, and people who stole them, and just how dangerous they (the people, not the mice) might be. I slipped, sort of shakily, into my seat.

P.J., who was already at her desk across the aisle, looked as if she was thinking, too. But I don't think she was thinking about danger. Suddenly, she leaned across the aisle. Mr. Collins had just begun a lecture on tardiness, but he was distracted for a moment by someone giggling in the front row. There was just time, before he turned our way again, for P.J. to whisper, "She knows something, Stacy. We find out at lunch!"

Only we didn't.
Because Monica never came back!
Instead, the school nurse came in to collect Monica's sweater and lunch box. She was being sent

home, the nurse told Mr. Collins, because she felt sick.

"Which is very peculiar," said P.J. when school was over and we were heading for the library just across the street.

"But anyone could get sick," I objected. "Look at Butch. He didn't come at all today."

P.J. snorted.

I knew what she was thinking. And I thought she was probably right. Butch Bigelow wasn't sick. He'd just invented some excuse to stay home so he wouldn't have to face P.J. and me, not to mention all those angry little kids he owed money to!

But Monica was different.

"I still say she's worried about the Brownies," I insisted.

But P.J. wasn't convinced. "Worried enough to get sick?" she said. "Worried enough to offer us a *bribe*?" She stopped, one foot on the library steps, one foot on the sidewalk. "No. She knows something. I'm sure of it. She was in the Bigelows' house yesterday. Maybe she saw something. Or someone. Anyway, we're going to find out . . . as soon as we finish in here."

And with that, she bounded up the library steps and disappeared through the front door.

There was nothing to do but follow. I caught up with her just as she reached the circulation desk.

"I'll be right with you," the librarian behind the counter said. She sounded frazzled, and in a moment, I understood why. She was trying to explain the new computerized checkout system to an angry patron.

"I'm sorry, sir," she was saying. "But the computer sends out overdue notices automatically."

"But I tell you, I'm going to return these books!"

the man exclaimed. "As soon as I find them. You shouldn't have sent me this!" He waved a computer printout in the air. "What's the world coming to? Where's the human dimension?"

The librarian looked as if she wanted to put her hands over her ears.

I sympathized with her. And with the man. Because I knew about those notices. My dad had gotten one for a book my brother, Victor, had lost—if you're a kid, they send the notice to your parents!—and he'd just about hit the ceiling. There's lots of legal stuff on them. It sounds like you're being sent to jail. The only way to stop the computer is to pay for the book before the notices go out. Then, if you find the book later, wedged behind your bed or in the dirty-clothes hamper or somewhere, you can get your money back.

The librarian was trying to explain all this, but the man wasn't interested.

"Computers!" he snorted, crumpling the notice up in a ball and throwing it down on the counter. "They'll be the end of us yet!"

And with that he stormed out the door. The librarian sank back in her chair with a sigh.

I thought we should give her a chance to recover before asking any questions. But P.J. wasn't about to wait. "We need some help," she said.

The librarian regarded us suspiciously. "Is it about the computer? Did you get a notice too?"

"No," P.J. said quickly. "It's about a crime! I mean . . ."

The startled look on the librarian's face warned P.J. to change her tack. "I mean," she said, "it's about a mouse. Mickey Mouse."

51

"Really?" The librarian sounded interested. "What about him?"

P.J. explained what we wanted.

As she spoke, the librarian looked more and more surprised. "Mickey Mouse banks," she said when P.J. had finished. "Old Mickey Mouse banks. Why yes, I *can* tell you where to find them. In a book called *The Collector's Companion.* I can even tell you the page. It's 194. But then maybe you'll tell *me* something." She looked at us curiously. "Why is there all this interest?"

"In banks?" P.J. asked.

"In Mickey Mouse banks," the librarian corrected. "You're the third request today!"

7

Suspects

This time it was P.J. who looked as if she could have been knocked over with a feather.

"We are?" she exclaimed.

Her eyes lit up.

Her nose gave a twitch.

She didn't need to nudge me in the side. I know an important development when I hear one. By the time she began firing questions at the librarian—"When were they here? Did you know them? Could you describe them?"—I'd whipped out my notebook and had my pencil ready.

The librarian looked a bit taken aback. I guess she wasn't used to being questioned, maybe I should say *interrogated*—that's what they call it in spy movies—by a skinny ten-year-old girl in a Mickey Mouse T-shirt.

But she must have been in a good mood, despite her run-in with the computer complainer, because she didn't say it was none of our business and send us packing. Instead, she frowned thoughtfully. "Well, I'm afraid I can't tell you who they were," she said, "because I don't usually work at this branch, so I'm not familiar with the people who come here. But I think I remember how they looked." She paused. "Let's see now. There was a man around lunchtime. Very nice. Wearing a suit and tie. He had brown hair and a mustache, I think."

Flipping to a clean page in my notebook, I made a quick sketch. Art isn't one of my specialties, but in this business you've got to be versatile—or in other words, able to do a lot of different things.

It was a pretty good drawing if I do say so myself.

P.J. peered over my shoulder. I could see that she was impressed. "Label it *Suspect A,*" she whispered before turning back to the librarian. "How about the other one?" she asked.

"Oh, a boy," the librarian replied. "He had curly hair and . . ."

"Curly hair," P.J. repeated. Her eyes narrowed. "Curly *brown* hair?"

"Why yes," the librarian said. "I believe so. He came in just after lunch and . . ."

But P.J. was no longer listening. The minute the librarian had said the boy had curly brown hair, she'd whirled around and grabbed me by the shoulders. "Did you hear that?" she said.

I must have looked stupid, because she gave me a shake, as if to make my brain start working.

"It's Butch!" she exclaimed. "I knew he wasn't sick! He must have found out about the bank. He's trying to solve his own case!"

She turned back to the librarian. "Where do we find *The Collector's Companion?*" she asked.

"In the reference section. The call number's 745.1," the librarian replied. "But what's this about a case? Has there been a crime?" She sounded alarmed. "Should I notify the police?"

"Don't worry," P.J. assured her. "They're working with us."

(Which was news to me!)

She dug into the pocket of her blue jeans, produced one of our cards, and presented it to the startled librarian. "Our number's there, in case you need to call," she said. Then she turned to me. "Come on." She pulled me toward the reference section.

I managed to murmur a hasty thank-you to the librarian.

(P.J. doesn't always remember things like that.)

And then, there we were, in front of number 745.1.

Quickly, P.J. pulled the book from the shelf and flipped to page 194.

There was a telltale chocolate stain in the margin (I could just imagine Butch Bigelow stuffing Mars bars into his mouth as he thumbed through the pages) and in the upper right-hand corner, a photograph that suddenly made my heart beat faster.

It was a picture of Mickey, or rather, of five different Mickeys—all with slots in the tops of their heads. They were lined up in a row, smiling for the photographer. The one at the far right looked just like the one on P.J.'s T-shirt. But the one on the far left was different somehow. Thinner. More mousey looking.

P.J. bent over the book. In a second, she let out a long, low whistle. "Read this," she said, forgetting to whisper. She pointed to the paragraph beneath the picture. It read:

Though it is difficult to assign a precise value, a mint condition Mickey Mouse coin bank manufactured between 1930 and 1938 (see bank at far left of photo) is probably worth around one thousand dollars.

I had a hard time understanding the first words, but the last ones were crystal clear. *Around one thousand dollars!*

"Could that be what Butch's bank is worth?" I gasped.

P.J., looking just as excited as I felt, grabbed my pencil and notepad.

"Between 1930 and 1938," she murmured. "So if it belonged to Butch's grandfather when he was a kid and if his grandfather is sixty now . . ." She jotted down some figures, did some adding and subtracting, and said, "Yes! That would just about do it! It must have been made around that time!"

I stared at the mouse in the photograph. I read the next paragraph. It said that after 1938 they'd changed Mickey's image. They'd made him look more human, more like the picture on P.J.'s T-shirt. That was why the earlier, mousier Mickeys were so valuable.

"No wonder someone wanted to steal it," P.J. murmured.

She picked up the book and checked the spine. "Reference. That means we can't check it out," she said, disappointed. "But we can copy it. Have you got a dime?"

I dug into my pocket and came up with ten cents. Somehow, I'd gotten the job of treasurer as well as secretary in this private eye business. I noticed that whenever money had to be produced, I was the one who produced it! But this was no time to argue.

P.J. took the dime and headed for the copy machine.

"Evidence," she explained as she put the book face down on the glass and made a photocopy of the page.

"Now, if we can just get hold of whoever's in charge of that Mickey Mouse collectors' show," she said, folding the photocopy and slipping it into her pocket.

"We'll tell them to be on the lookout for the bank and the man with the mustache, is that it?" I said.

"Exactly!" P.J. replied. "And meanwhile, we'll check those names on the list Mrs. Bigelow gave us. And Monica! I almost forgot about her. We'll find out what *she* knows. We'll be ahead of Butch there!"

"But P.J.—" I began.

I was going to say that beating Butch Bigelow wasn't the only thing at stake. There was a valuable bank with a valuable nickel inside. It seemed to me we'd have a better chance of finding both if we cooperated.

But P.J. didn't wait. She stuck *The Collector's Companion* back on the shelf and headed for the door before I could get a word out of my mouth. She was moving so fast that she almost ran into a couple of kids who were waiting their turn at the circulation desk.

"Hey, watch out," one of them said, nearly dropping the soccer ball he was carrying under one arm. I recognized Kevin Fisher, Monica's younger brother. He was a mess, as usual. And he seemed to be in trouble, as usual, too. This time it was over a lost library book.

"You're sure the computer won't send a notice?" I heard him saying to the librarian as I hurried after P.J.

"No, because you paid for it yesterday," the librarian replied.

(I'll bet she wished she had a tape-recorded message to answer all the computer questions she got.)

"Now if you just find that book and bring it in, I'll be able to give you your money back," she added as I went out the door after P.J., who was bounding down the steps two at a time.

"Where are you going?" I called. "What are we going to do?"

"We're going to find him," P.J. yelled back. "The man with the mustache. And we're going to find him before Butch Bigelow does!"

There was no time to ask questions.

Like how could she be so sure that the man with the mustache and the thief who'd taken Butch's bank were one and the same? After all, anyone could go to the library and look up Mickey Mouse stuff—though I had to admit it did seem suspicious!

But P.J. was going too fast for conversation. Besides, she had Butch on the brain! "Thinks he can solve his own case," she was saying. "Thinks he can put us out of business."

I didn't bother pointing out that *she* was the one who'd made the bet. When you've been P.J. Clover's best friend for years, you learn when to keep your mouth shut.

Instead, I hurried after her, keeping my opinions to myself. We were across the street in a flash. Passing in front of the school, I glanced up to see that the light in the principal's office was on. On the wall, I saw the poster I'd noticed before. But this time I could make out the picture. It was . . . a picture of Mickey Mouse!

"P.J.," I said, "wait. Look what the principal has on his . . ."

But P.J. didn't have time to hear about strange coincidences. She'd already dashed into the school-yard and grabbed her bike from the rack. Mine wasn't there because I'd driven to school with my mother. "Come on," she said, pulling to a halt beside me. "Hop on."

I hesitated. Then, I hopped. Because when P.J.'s in one of her hurry-up moods, there's nothing to do but hurry. I put the principal's poster out of my mind. After all, why shouldn't he have a picture of Mickey in his office? P.J. has one on her T-shirt. My brother, Victor, even has him grinning all over a set of bed sheets!

P.J. was pedaling fast and furiously in the direction of home and our clubhouse, and as she went, she out-lined her, or rather, *our* plan.

First we were going to find Monica's number in the phone book. Then we were going to call her and find out what she knew.

"She might have seen this guy who took the bank," P.J. speculated. "Maybe he's someone she knows and wants to cover up for. Or maybe . . ." She paused. "Yes! That could be it!"

"What?" I said. "What could be it?"

"A threat!" P.J. exclaimed, turning around and al-most running the bike into a tree.

She regained control in the nick of time.

"Suppose Monica saw the thief," she went on as I clutched her waist for dear life. "And suppose the thief saw her. What would he do? He'd threaten her, that's what! That would explain why she seemed so

60

scared. That would explain why she didn't want us to try to find the bank!"

A creepy feeling replaced the thrills and chills of the roller-coaster bike ride through the streets of Mill Creek. A picture of the thief—mustachioed, greasy, tough-looking—popped into my mind. What could he have said to Monica? *"Tell anyone you saw me, kid, and you'll be sorry!"* Something like that?

"Could be," P.J. panted. She was pedaling hard and more carefully now. "Anyway, we'll find out when we talk to her."

Next, she continued, we were going to locate whoever was in charge of the Mickey Mouse collectors' show. "There's probably a phone number at the end of that article," she said, "a number people can call for information." She swung her bike into her driveway, and we both jumped off.

"Now, if we can just find someone who has the rest of Sunday's paper . . ." She headed around the corner of the garage and into the backyard.

"P.J.!" I exclaimed, hurrying after her. "I'll bet we've got it. Victor's supposed to tie up the old papers and take them to the recycle, but he's always late."

I don't know whether she heard me or not, but all of a sudden, she stopped dead in her tracks.

I almost ran right smack into her. "What . . . ?" I began. But then I stopped.

Because I saw what she saw. Nailed to our clubhouse door, right over the picture of the eye, was a big, boldly lettered sign that read: OUT OF BUSINESS!!

Only one person could have done it. And as P.J. headed furiously across the yard, that person came out of our clubhouse door.

His curly brown hair was tousled. He didn't look sick, like someone who's spent the day home from school should look. He looked healthy. Healthy and angry.

"So!" he said. "You finally got here!"

"We— You—" P.J. sputtered. She's not usually at a loss for words, but I guess seeing Butch Bigelow— because that's who it was, of course—coming out of our clubhouse was too much for her.

"What are you doing?" she demanded, pulling herself together. "What do you mean out of business? What are you up to?"

"What am *I* up to?" Butch bounded down the clubhouse steps and planted himself in front of P.J. and me. "What are *you* up to? That's the question." He stuck out his chin.

He was holding a brown-paper lunch bag. It didn't look as if it contained sandwiches, though. It looked as if it contained something much heavier than peanut butter and jelly.

P.J. noticed the bag, too. "What's that?" she asked suspiciously.

Butch snorted. "As if you didn't know," he replied.

"Huh?" said P.J. She stopped looking angry and started looking confused.

I stole a quick glance at Butch's eyes. I'd read somewhere that when someone goes bananas, their pupils get small. But Butch's seemed the same as ever.

"Come on," he said. "You had me fooled, showing up just after the police, flashing your card around. But I'm onto you now."

"You're what?" P.J. said. She looked as if she'd wandered into the middle of a wacky movie and was trying to figure out what was going on. "What are you talking about?"

"I'm talking about this!" Butch exclaimed, opening the paper bag and reaching inside. "Don't act innocent. This case is solved!"

"Solved? You mean . . ." I stared at the bag. Could it contain . . . ? Had Butch actually found . . . ?

"Give me that!" P.J. said. She snatched the bag out of Butch's hand and reached inside.

I caught my breath. "Is it the bank?" I asked.

In reply, P.J. pulled a fat, pink, curly-tailed something from the bag. It had a grin on its face and a slot in its back. It was a bank, all right. But it wasn't a mouse. It was a pig!

Taped to its side was a note. P.J. ripped it off.

"You don't have to read it," Butch snorted. "You know what it says. You wrote it."

P.J. paid no attention. She stared at the note. Her eyes opened wide, and her nose gave a twitch.

"Stacy," she said, "look at this!"

8

I Had To Do It!

I leaned over her shoulder. The note was typed. It said:

SORRY. BUT I HAD TO DO IT!

"Where'd you get this?" I heard P.J. demand as an uneasy feeling crept over me. The note sounded like something you'd read about in the newspapers. Like something left by a mad bomber, or a baby snatcher, or someone who'd tried to shoot the president.

"Where'd I— Oh, come on," Butch said. "Give up. I know you just wanted to get even with me. I know you staged this whole thing."

"We *what?*" I exclaimed. "Butch, are you crazy? We didn't . . ."

But Butch wasn't listening. He had his old spirit back, and he wasn't about to stop. "You went one step too far when you left old porky here on my doorstep," he said. "That's when I—"

"On your doorstep?" P.J. interrupted. "Is that where you found it?"

"Yeah," Butch said. For the first time since he'd come out of our clubhouse, he sounded uncertain. "On the step where you left it."

P.J. shook her head. "Butch," she said solemnly. "We didn't leave this."

"We never saw it before," I said.

"You . . . you didn't?" Butch looked from P.J. to me and then back to P.J. again.

"No," P.J. said. "Honest. And we didn't stage any fake robbery either."

I could see that Butch wanted to object. That he wanted to say she was lying. But I could also see that he knew she was telling the truth.

"You mean you don't have my bank?" he said finally. "You didn't take it just to get even with me? You don't have the nickel?"

"No!" P.J. replied. "Use your head. We couldn't have taken it. We were in school all day yesterday. And after that we were right here, dealing with all those phony cases you sent us. We've got tons of witnesses. We couldn't have taken your bank. We didn't know about the nickel. And we wouldn't have any reason for leaving a pig on your doorstep."

Butch gulped. He looked like someone who'd just missed catching a life preserver. He stared at the fat pink piggy bank and at the note that P.J. still held in her hands. "Then . . . then who . . . ?" he said.

"I don't know," P.J. replied, "but we're going to find out." She stepped over to the clubhouse and ripped Butch's Out of Business sign from the door. "So let's not play any more games. Just tell us, when did you find this? Before you went to the library or after?"

Now, it was Butch's turn to look confused. "The library?" he said. "I didn't go to the library."

P.J. stared at him. "You didn't? You mean you're not the boy with the curly hair?"

Butch's hand went up to his head. He patted his hair as if to make sure it was still curly. But his face was a blank.

P.J. pulled the page she'd copied from *The Collector's Companion* out of her pocket. "You mean you don't know anything about this?" she asked.

Butch stared at the page. His face was still blank. Then, a look of recognition came into his eyes. "Hey, that's my bank," he said, pointing to the mousey-looking Mickey at the far left of the photo. "It was sort of funny-looking like that and . . ."

He stopped. His eyes opened wider, and then they just about popped out of his head. "A thousand bucks," he gasped. "Is this some kind of a joke?"

"No," P.J. replied. "It's true. We thought you knew. We thought you were at the library checking it out."

Butch stared at the picture of the five Mickeys. "That old bank," he murmured. "That beat-up old thing." He frowned. "But . . . but how about this?" he said, taking the grinning pink pig back from P.J. "Where does this fit in?"

That was a good question. And for once P.J. Clover didn't have an answer. "I don't know," she admitted. "Unless . . . unless . . . Yes. That could be it." She looked at Butch and me excitedly. "Suppose this thief, whoever he is, felt bad about taking a kid's bank. Suppose he felt so bad that he snuck back and left *this* as a replacement."

"This?" Butch looked at the piggy. "A replacement? For a thousand-dollar bank?"

I could see what he meant. The pig was cute. But not *that* cute. Then, another thought struck me. I took the bank and gave it a shake. There was no jingle.

"P.J.," I said, "there's no money in here. If the thief felt sorry for Butch and was going to go to all the trouble of leaving this on his doorstep, wouldn't he have put the money inside? I mean, even supposing he knew that nickel was valuable, he could have kept that and returned the rest."

"That's right," Butch agreed. "And what about the note? What about all that 'I had to do it' stuff? Why would someone *have* to steal my bank? Especially on . . ." He paused and a pained expression came over his face. "Especially on the day I dropped my dad's nickel in it?"

"But the thief wouldn't have known that," P.J. pointed out. "And maybe he really did need it. Maybe he was out of a job. Or maybe one of his kids needed an operation. Or . . ."

She stopped herself. Maybe she realized she was letting her imagination run away with her!

"Anyway, we're going to find it!" she said. "Listen, Butch . . ."

(For the first time in my life, I heard her talking to him like a normal human being.)

"We think whoever stole your bank is going to take it to a Mickey Mouse collectors' show that's being held in the city tomorrow. Now, if we just go there . . ."

Butch shook his head. He looked more miserable than ever before. "It won't work," he groaned.

"What do you mean?" P.J. said.

"I mean, tomorrow's too late," he replied. "That's why I jumped at the idea that you'd cooked this whole thing up. I *wanted* to believe it. I *wanted* you to have the money."

He ran his hand through his hair. For a moment I didn't think he was going to go on. But finally he managed to get the words out. "You see, there's been a change of plans," he said desperately. "My dad's coming home tonight. At eight thirty!"

"But he won't go looking for his nickel right away," said P.J.

"Oh, yes, he will," replied Butch. "Because he's bringing a friend home with him. A coin collecting friend who's interested in buying that nickel!"

At that disturbing news, P.J. spun into action.

"Stacy," she commanded. "Go home. Get the Sunday paper with the article about the collectors' show in it, and bring it back here. Butch, come with me. We're going to call Monica Fisher. She knows something and—"

I didn't wait to hear the rest.

My house is just down the block from P.J.'s, and by the time she finished her sentence, I was halfway there. My mind was racing as fast as my feet.

First of all I was feeling sorry for Butch. Then I was wondering who the boy with the curly hair in the library had been. And finally I was trying to figure out what that note taped to the fat pink pig could mean. "I had to do it!" It didn't sound like something an ordinary thief would write. It was weird. Crazy. Scary even.

I was thinking so hard I almost walked right past my house.

"Hey!" my brother, Victor, called. "Come back to earth."

He was kneeling on the driveway tying newspapers into bundles. "Where's Sunday's?" I said, remembering what I'd come for. "You didn't take it to the recycle yet, did you?"

"No way," Victor replied with a groan. "It's over there." He pointed to the top of a huge stack of untied papers. "How come this isn't your job?"

I didn't have time to remind him that he'd picked tying over drying (dishes, that is) when the jobs were handed out.

I headed for the stack and began to dig through the papers. In a moment I'd found the section P.J. had torn the article from. MILLION-DOLLAR MOUSE! The headline still gave me goosebumps.

I glanced at the last line of the column: "Continued on page 33."

Quickly, I flipped through the pages. I folded the paper back and all at once, a face—a familiar face—leaped out at me. It was a man with a mustache!

NEW MILL CREEK RESIDENT HAS MANIA FOR MICKEY, the caption beneath the photograph read. And then, a quote: "I know it's crazy, but I can't seem to help myself. Whenever I see a Mickey Mouse, I *have* to have it!"

I don't know if there was a phone number at the end of the column. I don't know what else the article said. Because all I could do was stare at that face. I remembered the list I'd made at the Bigelows' house yesterday. His name had been on it. I didn't need to take out my notebook to check. I could see it in my mind's eye as clear as day. Number two, Mr.—

"Hey!" Victor said, leaning over my shoulder to see what I was staring at. "Isn't that Mr. McMurphy? The new principal of Park School?"

I sat back on my heels.

"What's the matter?" Victor asked. "You look like you just stumbled over a corpse."

I wouldn't have put it that way, but as Victor spoke, I realized that's exactly how I felt!

It couldn't be true, and yet . . . What had my mother said? She'd been chattering away about him this morning as we carried the stuff for Parent Night into the auditorium.

"Such an interesting hobby . . . Has his whole office full . . ."

I remembered the poster I'd seen on the wall.

She must have been about to say "of Mickey Mouse stuff" when she was interrupted by the bell.

She'd been talking about him last night at dinner, too. Victor and I had been arguing about clearing the table, but I seemed to remember her saying that he came from another school district, that no one knew much about him, that he'd been at our house getting acquainted and—

Suddenly, I thought of something.

"Victor," I said. "Your Mickey Mouse sheets—are they on your bed?"

"How should I know," Victor replied. "I sleep with my eyes closed." He grinned at his own cleverness.

I didn't. Instead, I tore the column with the picture on it out of the paper, stuffed it into my pocket, and headed for the house.

"Hey, what's up?" I heard Victor shouting as I bounded up the stairs to his room.

Quickly, I tore the covers from his bed. Pink and blue butterflies. No wonder he didn't remember! But no Mickey.

I raced down the hall and threw open the doors to the linen closet. Stripes, plaids, whites, and more butterflies greeted my eyes. But no Mickey.

I picked up the lid of the dirty-clothes hamper. There were Victor's blue jeans, my dad's jogging suit, a pair of pink pajamas. No Mickey.

With my heart pounding, I ran down to the laundry room, opened the dryer, and dug through the load inside. White towels, checked tablecloth, underpants, socks. But still no Mickey.

They were gone. That was all there was to it. Victor's sheets with Mickey Mouse grinning all over them were as gone as Butch Bigelow's bank!

9

I Know Who Did It

I don't know how I got back to the clubhouse. I must have walked—or run—but I don't remember. All I remember is thinking about that face in the newspaper. About that quote: *"I know it's crazy, but I can't seem to help myself. Whenever I see a Mickey Mouse, I have to have it!"* And how it echoed the words of the note taped to the fat pink pig: *Sorry. But I had to do it!*

I climbed the clubhouse steps and threw open the door.

P.J. and Butch were sitting at the card table. Butch had an open phone book in front of him. P.J. had her hand on the phone. (We can bring the phone out from the Clovers' house and in through the clubhouse window—at least whenever P.J.'s mother's not around.) The file folders full of phony cases were stacked up between them. The map of Mill Creek dotted with pushpins still hung on the wall. But neither Butch nor P.J. seemed to notice.

In fact, P.J. hardly looked up when I came in the door. "How many more are there?" she was saying to Butch, who was running his finger down a column in the phone book, counting under his breath. "We've called eight different Fishers already," she explained, glancing in my direction. "I never knew there were so many in Mill Creek. If we only knew her father's name, we'd . . ."

Suddenly she stopped. She looked at me again. Then she looked harder.

I don't know what she saw because there's no mirror in the clubhouse, but whatever it was it must have been alarming.

"Stacy, what happened?" she said, jumping up from her seat behind the card table. "What's wrong?"

I didn't know what to say. I didn't know how to put it into words. I wished it weren't true. But there was no way around it.

"I think . . ." I began. My voice came out in a squeaky sort of whisper. "I know who did it!"

"It can't be," Butch said when I'd managed to choke out the name. "I don't believe it."

"Why not?" exclaimed P.J. She'd stood silently listening as I spilled out my suspicions. But now she began to pace back and forth across the clubhouse floor. She had the column I'd torn from the newspaper in one hand and the column she'd torn out in the other.

"It would explain a lot of things," she said, looking at the photograph of the principal's mustachioed face. "Like that note. And Monica. You saw how she looked when he came into the hall. You know how she always tries to stay in good with the teachers. If she saw him take it, she'd be sure to cover up. Though from the way she acted, I still think she was threatened."

"But P.J., he didn't even recognize her," I objected. It was one thing to suspect the principal of taking the bank because of some uncontrollable urge, but threatening Monica? I didn't even want to think of it.

"I don't mean that he meant to," P.J. said quickly. "Maybe when this . . . this mania comes over him, he goes into sort of a trance. He's not himself."

"Like Dr. Jekyll and Mr. Hyde," Butch suggested.

"Exactly!" P.J. agreed.

(Which didn't make me feel any better.)

"Well, I still can't believe it," Butch said. "The principal of a school just wouldn't—"

But before he could finish his sentence, there was a knock on the door.

P.J., forgetting to use the peephole, swung it open.

For a second I thought we'd slipped back in time. Because there was a boy—the very same boy who'd given Butch's scheme away yesterday—standing on the steps.

He didn't look nervous this time though. He looked confident. "I've got a case for the eye," he said boldly.

P.J. looked at Butch suspiciously.

"Now wait a second, I didn't . . ." he protested.

"It's a real one this time," the boy said. "It's my Mick—"

"Forget it," P.J. interrupted. "We don't have time to . . . Wait! Were you going to say your Mickey—?"

"That's right," the boy replied eagerly. "My Mickey Mouse cookie jar. It was in the kitchen, and now it's gone. It didn't have any cookies in it, but—"

"Forget about the cookies!" P.J. exclaimed, grabbing the startled boy by the shoulders. "Just tell us, is your mother in the P.T.A.?"

"She is," Butch said, stepping in before the boy had a chance to reply. "She's the treasurer. She goes to meetings with my mom."

P.J.'s nose gave a twitch. She gave the boy a shake. "Someone visited her yesterday, didn't they?" she said.

"No. I mean . . ." The boy squirmed in her grasp. He looked as if he wished he'd never knocked on the door. "I mean, just a couple of people. My aunt came over and—"

"And the new principal of Park School?"

At that, the boy stopped squirming. He looked at P.J. with undisguised admiration. She might have just pulled a rabbit out of a hat.

"Hey, you really are a good detective," he said. "How did you know—"

P.J. didn't wait for him to finish. "Still think he's innocent?" she said, letting the boy go and turning to Butch.

"I . . . I guess not," he replied. "It's hard to believe, but . . ." He let his voice trail off.

I felt my heart sink.

"Well, what are we waiting for?" said P.J. "Let's go!"

At first, I thought we were going straight to the police. But P.J. had other plans.

"There's no time for that," she said, heading out of the clubhouse and across the backyard with Butch and me at her heels.

(The boy with the missing cookie jar was left standing, looking baffled, on our clubhouse steps.)

"It would take days to convince *them,* and Butch needs his bank back *now.*"

"So what do we do?" asked Butch, panting slightly from trying to keep up. "Just go take it?"

"Exactly!" P.J. replied.

I don't think it was the answer Butch had expected. After all, he'd never worked with P.J. Clover before! He looked shocked. "You mean sneak into his office at school and—"

"Right!" P.J. said. "That's where the article in the newspaper said he keeps his collection. So all we have to do is get in there and—"

"But P.J., that's—"

"Stealing" is what I was going to say.

But P.J. didn't give me a chance.

"Setting things right, that's what it is," she said. She turned to Butch. "Can you identify your bank?" she asked.

"Of course," he replied. "It's got my grandfather's name on the bottom. But do you really think we should—"

P.J. cut him off. "Perfect!" she pronounced. She stopped on the driveway beside her bike. "Then there won't be any doubt about it. Now listen, here's my plan. . . ."

10

A Mouse Paradise

It would never have worked if it hadn't been Parent Night, because on any other night Park School would have been locked up. But now, as we cut across the playground, the school loomed ahead of us, its front doors thrown open, the auditorium ablaze with light.

It was seven o'clock.

The hour and a half that had passed since P.J. unfolded her plan seemed like the longest I'd ever spent.

"Couldn't we just go now and get it over with?" I'd asked.

But P.J. was adamant, which means she wouldn't be budged. "We've got to wait until it's dark," she insisted. "We've got to wait until everyone's busy with Parent Night stuff. Then we can sneak in without being noticed."

So I'd gone home and eaten supper. P.J. and Butch had gone to their houses, too. After supper, I'd headed straight for my room. Luckily, my mother had already left for school. She had to finish setting up the decorations and refreshments in the auditorium. My father and Victor were playing a hot game of Space Invaders in the den. No one noticed when P.J. whistled outside my window or when I slipped out the back door to join her and Butch on the sidewalk outside.

"Ready?" she whispered.

"I . . . I guess so," I said. The truth was, I didn't think I'd ever be ready to break into the principal's office at Park School! Butch looked worried, too, but he didn't say anything. I guess he'd found out what I'd known all along. Namely, that once P.J. Clover gets an idea there's no stopping her. There was nothing for us to do but hurry along the blocks toward school until now, here we were, almost at the door.

I glanced nervously around. Across the street I could see that the library was still open. I wondered if the same librarian was at the desk, explaining the computer system to kids like Kevin Fisher. I wondered if . . .

But then I stopped myself.

I'd been wondering too much. All the way to the school I'd been wondering. About things like why the principal hadn't put Butch's money in the piggy bank he'd left on the doorstep.

("Forgot to," said P.J. confidently.)

And why he'd been looking up the value of banks in *The Collector's Companion* if all he was interested in was *having* Mickey Mouse stuff, not selling it.

("Curiosity," P.J. replied, though that time she hadn't sounded quite so sure of herself.)

And who the boy with the curly hair really was.

P.J. didn't have an answer for that. "But even in Nancy Drew there's always a few things that don't get explained," she said. So I stopped asking questions. It was making my head ache anyway.

We ducked past the bike rack and headed for the side door. "Now, let's get this straight," Butch whispered. "We sneak in there, get the bank—"

"*If* it's there," I interrupted. Though I was the one who'd started it all, I still couldn't help hoping I'd been wrong.

"*If* it's there," Butch corrected himself. "We take it, and then we call the police?"

"Right," said P.J. "Because then we'll have evidence. They'll have to believe us."

"But P.J.," I objected. A picture of the new principal sweating it out under hot lights at the Mill Creek police station had suddenly popped into my mind. "Don't you think we could just tell our parents or the P.T.A. or something? Do we have to call the police?"

"No," P.J. replied, "we don't." She stopped and pointed to the street beside the school. "We don't have to call them, because they're already here!"

I turned to see a police car parked by the curb. Its lights were off, and no one was in it.

"Maybe they're here because of Parent Night," Butch said.

P.J. nodded. "Maybe. Anyway, we'll have to be careful," she warned, heading for the steps leading to the side door of the school. "Remember, they're armed!"

That did it. My knees, which had been feeling pretty shaky, suddenly turned to jelly. "P.J.," I said. "We can't . . ." But she and Butch were already inside.

By the time I got through the door they were disappearing down the dimly lit hall. I couldn't call them back. Someone would be sure to hear. Taking a deep breath and trying to make my heart stop pounding, I moved cautiously through the door and into the hallway.

The sound of people laughing and talking was coming from the auditorium. The principal's office lay just beyond the auditorium around a bend in the hall. I caught sight of P.J. and Butch. They had ducked into a doorway just as a group of parents crossed the hall.

P.J. turned and gestured for me to follow. Then she and Butch slipped past the lighted auditorium and scurried down the darkened hall on the other side.

Hugging the wall, I hurried after them. The auditorium was already full of people. As I ducked past, I caught a glimpse of my mother standing behind the refreshment table. She'd decorated it with the vase and dried leaves I'd carried in from the car. Some kind of statue was standing at one end, and the whole thing was covered with a white cloth dotted with brightly colored pictures.

Suddenly I saw Monica Fisher. She was standing just inside the auditorium door, staring down the hallway where P.J. and Butch had just disappeared. A red badge marked her as one of the student volunteers for Parent Night. Still, it seemed strange to see her. If she was as scared of the new principal as P.J. thought she was, it didn't make sense for her to come back to school.

Then I remembered something. In the confusion of finding the story in the paper and making plans, we'd never gotten around to calling Monica.

I glanced down the hall. P.J. was nowhere in sight. I turned back to the auditorium. But now Monica had disappeared, too. I hesitated, not sure if I should try to go in after her, but the sight of Mr. Collins coming across the hall to the auditorium made up my mind. Quickly, I flattened myself against the wall and edged down the hallway.

I snuck around the corner and saw P.J. and Butch hiding in the alcove by the drinking fountain across from one of the doors to the principal's office.

The hallway was unlit. The rippled glass at the top of the office door showed that the room inside was dark too.

P.J. gestured to me impatiently. "Where have you been?" she whispered.

Butch stepped cautiously across the hall and put his hand on the knob of the office door. He gave it a turn.

"P.J., wait," I whispered. "I just saw—"

But the sound of footsteps coming from the direction of the auditorium made all of us jump. There was no time to say anything about Monica. No time to say anything at all. Butch had pulled the door open, and in a second we were inside.

For a moment none of us moved. It was dark. The footsteps had stopped. There was no sound at all except for the thumping of my heart, and I don't think anyone else could hear that!

Butch pulled a tiny pencil-shaped flashlight from his pocket and clicked it on. The beam was small but bright.

"Don't aim it too high," P.J. whispered. The tremor in her voice told me that *I* wasn't the only one who was nervous. "We don't want anyone to know we're here."

Muttering something about not being stupid, Butch kept the beam low and moved it slowly around the room.

All at once, I wished I could see more. Because even in the darkness I could tell that the office was full of interesting things. There was the poster of Mickey that I'd seen through the window. A clock in the shape of a Mickey Mouse watch hung beside it. All kinds of objects covered the shelves and desk.

Butch's light picked them out, one by one. A set of bookends, a pencil holder, the base of a lamp—all in the shape of Mickey Mouse.

It was a regular mouse paradise. And seeing it, I almost forgot why we were there. I was even thinking how great it was for Park School to have a principal with an office like this when all at once Butch's light stopped moving.

"That's it!" he whispered. "That's my bank!"

I returned to earth with a jolt.

The beam was aimed at a ceramic figure of Mickey perched on the desk. I recognized it right away. It was just like the picture in *The Collector's Companion*. It was mousier looking than most of the other Mickeys in the office, and it had a slot in the top of its head.

So it was true. The new principal *was* a thief!

"Careful," P.J. warned as Butch reached out to take the bank.

His hand was almost on it when a sound came from the hall.

"Wait. Someone's coming," P.J. whispered. "Quick, hide!"

There was just time, just barely time, for the three of us to dive behind the desk.

Butch switched off the flashlight as the door from the hall slowly opened.

I hardly dared breathe. I waited for the lights to be switched on, for someone to come around the desk, for someone to discover us crouched there in the dark. But none of that happened.

The lights stayed off. No one came around the desk. For a moment it seemed as if a ghost must have entered the office. Then I heard footsteps moving cautiously across the floor.

They were light, as if they were made by someone no bigger than I was. I scrunched down, trying to see from under the desk, when all at once something moved. Not *in* the office, but outside it. On the other side of the glass door leading not to the hall, but to the school secretary's office.

A tall, thin figure was suddenly silhouetted in the glass. His head was large and lumpy. No. Not lumpy. Curly. I caught my breath. It was a boy—a boy with curly hair!

A shiver traveled down my back as the shadowy figure reached out. He turned the knob on the door. Then something brushed past me like a ghost.

I opened my mouth to scream, but P.J., who heard me draw in my breath, clapped her hand over it. "Sh," she hissed as the curly-haired boy opened the door and stepped into the room.

A Robbery!

There was a click, as of a flashlight being turned on, and then a beam of light began to trace its way slowly around the room.

A faint whimper came from behind me, and I realized that whatever had brushed past me wasn't ghostly. It was real. Whoever had come into the office through the hall door had dived behind the desk just as we had. Now he or she was hiding there with us!

I tried to turn around, but the squeak of a floorboard stopped me. Luckily, the curly-haired boy was too intent on what he was doing to notice.

And what was he doing?

Forgetting about whoever was behind me, I scrunched down again. This time I had a clear view of the office from under the desk. It was dark, of course. But in the beam of the flashlight I could see most of what was happening. The boy was taking Mickey Mouse things from the shelves and bookcases and dropping them into a sack. It was a robbery!

P.J.'s hand, as cold as ice, gripped my arm as the flashlight worked its way closer. My heart was beating so hard I was sure the thief could hear it. Was he armed? Should we stay where we were? Should we try to stop him?

My head was swimming. I couldn't think. Then all at once everything was decided.

The light had stopped moving. It was shining down on the top of the desk—just about where Butch Bigelow's bank was standing.

I sensed rather than saw the thief's hand reach out.

Suddenly, there was a bellow of rage. "Stop that!" Butch Bigelow leaped to his feet behind the desk. "That's mine!" he cried.

P.J. and I scrambled to our feet.

The flashlight dropped to the floor.

Someone screamed.

And the office was bathed in light. "Police," a deep voice barked. "Don't anybody move!"

Nobody did. Nobody could. Everybody was too confused.

There was Butch, his hand on the bank. There was the thief, a young man, not a boy—though I suppose he might have seemed like a boy to the middle-aged librarian. There was P.J. And me. Staring into the eyes of the very same two officers who'd been at Butch Bigelow's house yesterday.

There was someone else, too. A man with a mustache! He was standing beside the police. "That's the one," he said, pointing to the young man with the curly hair. "That's the young man I saw looking in the window this morning. But what are you three doing in here?"

The new principal looked from P.J. to Butch to me and then back to P.J. again. His eyes rested on the picture of Mickey grinning from the front of her T-shirt. But he didn't smile as he had earlier in the day.

"No, it can't be," he said, shaking his head in disbelief. "Are you—students of Park School—in on this too?"

P.J. opened her mouth to speak, but Butch beat her to it.

"Us!" he exclaimed. "You mean, you think that we . . . and this guy . . . ?" He gestured to the curly-haired young man standing beside him, his head hanging morosely, the sack of Mickey Mouse loot in his hands. "You think we . . . ?"

The principal shook his head sadly. "I guess I never should have told that reporter from the newspaper about my collection being in here," he said to the police. "It was just too tempting. I know what it's like, of course, but—"

"*You* know what it's like?" This time it was P.J. who interrupted. "I'll say you do!" She grabbed the Mickey Mouse bank from the desk and turned to the policemen, who were standing there looking as if they didn't know what had hit them. "*This* is the bank that was stolen from my client's room yesterday!" she announced.

"Stolen?" The principal's eyebrows shot up. "What do you mean? That bank is mine."

"Then why," said P.J., "does it have the name of my client's grandfather on the bottom?"

And with that, she turned the bank over.

The police, the principal, Butch Bigelow, myself, and even the thief leaned forward to see.

90

It would have been embarrassing if there'd been no name. But there was. It was scratched in a boyish sort of handwriting into the bottom of the bank.

Bertram Bigelow

"Is that your grandfather's name?" P.J. asked Butch.

"Yeah," Butch replied. "Bertram Bigelow, same as . . ." He stopped himself before the word *mine* could slip out of his mouth. Butch does not like to remind people that his real name is Bertram.

"Yeah," he backtracked. "It's his all right." He stuck his chin out as if daring someone to challenge it.

But no one did.

Instead, the police looked questioningly at the principal.

And the principal looked at the bank.

"I don't understand," he murmured, a bewildered expression on his face. "I have a bank just like this. It was here on my desk. At least, I thought it was. I even went to the library this afternoon because I wanted to check . . ."

But before he could say another word, a sound—a stifled sort of moan—came from behind the desk. I'd forgotten all about the other intruder in the principal's office!

The police were right on the ball. "Come out of there," one of them (the one who'd compared P.J. and me to the Lone Ranger and Tonto) commanded.

Slowly, a head covered with wavy hair held back by a barrette with a metal disk on it rose from behind the desk. Its owner looked frightened. More frightened than she'd looked this morning in the hall outside our classroom. More frightened than *I'd* felt when she'd brushed past me like a ghost a few minutes before.

"Monica Fisher!" I exclaimed.

"What are *you* doing here?" said Butch.

Monica looked as if she wanted to bolt out the door. "I—I—" she stammered. The badge pinned to her chest quivered.

"All right, take it easy," the policeman said. "Just tell us whether you know something about this—"

But Butch jumped in before Monica had a chance to open her mouth. "You bet she does," he said. "I don't know what she's doing here, but she knows plenty." He turned to Monica. "Tell them," he said, shooting a hard look at the principal. "There's nothing to be scared of now. Tell them who took it."

"But, I . . ." Monica murmured. "I didn't . . . I mean, I did. . . ." Suddenly, her lip began to tremble. "But I didn't mean to," she said. "It was a mistake. It was all a mistake." And at that, the floodgates gave way. Tears began to stream down her plump cheeks.

Then P.J., who had been staring, not at Monica's face, but at her hair—or rather, at the barrette that held back her hair—let out a cry.

She dug into her pocket and pulled out the metal disk with the picture of Mickey Mouse that she'd found on Butch Bigelow's floor. "Monica, is this yours?" she said.

Instinctively, Monica reached up to touch the barrette in her hair. And, for the first time, I noticed that it had a picture on it. A brightly colored picture enameled on the metal disk. A picture of Mickey . . . No, I was wrong. It wasn't Mickey. It was Minnie. Minnie Mouse.

Beside the disk was an empty space. I could see that another disk had been attached to it. Could it have been a disk with a picture of Mickey?

P.J. was frowning. What was she thinking? That Monica had been in Butch's room yesterday? That she'd seen the principal?

But from the jumble of words Monica had just stammered out it didn't sound as if she had. It sounded as if . . .

I looked at P.J. again. Was she thinking—*could* she be thinking—that *Monica* was the one who . . . ? But no. It couldn't be. It didn't make sense.

"Monica," P.J. said softly. "Why were you in Butch's room yesterday?"

"I . . ." Monica began. She looked helplessly from P.J. to the principal to the police. Everyone was waiting for her reply, but P.J. didn't give her a chance.

"How did Butch's bank get into this office?" she pressed. "Why are you here now? Who—?"

But Monica had had enough.

"Stop!" she exclaimed.

"Then tell us," P.J. insisted.

"All right," Monica said. "All right." Her lip trembled. She took a breath. She looked as if a weight had suddenly been lifted from her shoulders. Though her eyes were full of tears, she was standing taller. Then, "I put it here," she said. "But there was no other way. I had to do it. I *had* to!"

If you're feeling confused right now, it's nothing to what *I* felt standing there in that office looking at Monica's tearstained face.

"You?" I said. "But . . . but why?"

"Because I *had* to," Monica repeated. "When I saw it standing there in Butch's room looking just like . . . just like . . ." She seemed to choke on the words.

"Just like the one in this office," P.J. suggested.

For a moment I didn't know what she was talking about. Then I realized. The principal had a bank just like Butch's. That's what he'd said. It had been right here on his desk. But I didn't see what that had to do with Monica. I didn't see what that had to do with her taking Butch's bank.

"It was a mistake," she moaned. "I was here in the office bringing a note from Mr. Collins. I picked it up. Just to look, and . . ." Her lip trembled again. "But it was an accident. It was all an accident."

And once again—before anyone could step in and say "*What* was an accident?"—Monica broke down in tears.

This time the principal stepped forward to comfort her. "Now, now," he said. "Nothing could be that terrible." He put his hand on her shoulder, and Monica's sobs subsided a bit.

The taller of the two police officers turned to the principal. "This bank business doesn't sound like a matter for the law," he said. "So if it's all right with you, we'll take this fellow"—he indicated the thief with the curly hair—"down to the station and start filling out our report."

"Yes," Mr. McMurphy agreed. "Yes, of course. I think I can handle this myself."

"We'll call if we need a statement from you," the other officer said as they ushered the thief out the door. "And thanks," he added, nodding to P.J. and

94

Butch and me. "We knew this guy was planning something, but if you hadn't been here making so much noise we might not have caught him in the act."

It was a compliment, of a sort, but there was no time to enjoy it. Because the minute the police were out the door, the principal got down to business.

"All right, I want some explanations," he said.

P.J. opened her mouth. I could see that she was itching to explain. But the principal didn't want to hear from *her*. He wanted to hear from Monica.

"Now if I understand this right," he said, kindly but firmly, "you took this boy's bank from his room. And then you put it in my office. Why?"

Monica struggled, trying to choke back her tears. "Because . . . because I . . ."

"Well?" the principal said.

"Because I broke it!" Monica blurted out. "Your bank. The one that was here on your desk. I . . ."

"You broke it?" Butch exclaimed. "A thousand-dollar bank?"

Monica looked shocked. "A thousand . . ." she began.

"Now wait a minute," the principal interrupted. "Mine wasn't worth that. It was only a copy. But I've always wanted to own a real one. That's why I was checking the price in the library."

Just like the curly-haired young man, I thought. He'd seen the bank through the window of the office and then he'd checked it out to see if it was worth taking!

"But Monica," I said. "Why didn't you just tell someone what happened? I mean, anyone can break something. Anyone can make a mistake."

"But not me!" Monica exclaimed. "I'm not like Kevin. I don't get into trouble. I thought if I just put Butch's bank in here no one would ever know. Then when I heard that you were looking for it, I got worried. And when I saw you at school tonight, everything got mixed up. I thought I'd better sneak in here and get it back and hide it before you found it. I thought that . . ." And once again, tears started to run down her cheeks.

Butch squirmed uncomfortably.

I looked at P.J. She didn't look eager anymore. She looked sad. I was sure we were thinking the same thing. Anyone who felt as Monica did—anyone who would commit a crime just to cover up a simple human mistake—needed help.

The principal must have thought so, too. Of course, being new, he didn't know anything about Monica or her brother, Kevin, or the rest of her family. But I think he was planning to find out.

"All right," he said, patting Monica's shoulder. "That's enough for now. You've explained things. Now, how about going down to the auditorium? They have a refreshment table and there'll be plenty of time later for . . ."

"Hey!" Butch interrupted. "Wait! I almost forgot. My money!" He grabbed the bank from P.J.'s hands.

The moment he did, I knew something was wrong.

It didn't jingle.

Butch gave it a shake. It still didn't jingle. "Where is it?" he asked, turning to Monica. "Where's my money?"

Monica looked baffled. "Money?" she said. "But there wasn't any money in your bank."

12

The Three-legged Buffalo

"No money?" Butch said. "What do you mean, no money?"

"There wasn't any," Monica insisted. "If there was I would have given it back when I . . ."

She meant when she'd left the pink pig on Butch's doorstep, but I guess she didn't want to say it. I guess she thought her behavior looked foolish enough already.

Butch wasn't thinking about pigs, though. He was thinking about three-legged buffaloes. "But what happened to it? It was in here. I know it was." He gave the bank another shake.

"Wait a second!" P.J. cried. "Give me that." She grabbed the bank from Butch. "There *is* something inside. I heard it rattle."

She held the bank up and shook it herself. This time I heard it too. Not coins. Something softer.

Quickly, P.J. turned the bank over and unscrewed the bottom. "It's some kind of note," she said, reaching inside and pulling out a scrap of paper.

Everyone, Mr. McMurphy included, leaned over her shoulder.

"'I.O.U.,'" P.J. began, reading the messy handwriting on the note.

Suddenly, Monica turned pale. "Kevin," she gasped. "That's Kevin's handwriting."

"Your brother?" Butch said. "Hey! Wait a minute. He was one of the guys that came by with my friends to get me to play soccer! He must have seen . . ."

"'Six dollars and thirty-eight cents,'" Monica interrupted, reading the rest of the note. "Oh, no! Why didn't I give it to him?"

"What are you talking about?" P.J. said.

"Kevin," Monica groaned. "He lost a library book. The computer at the library was going to send a notice home if he didn't pay for it. He asked me to loan him the money, but I wouldn't, so . . ."

"So he took Butch's money and left this I.O.U.!" P.J. exclaimed. "And then later, you came along and took the bank. Oh, wow!" she said. "Who would have believed it? A *double* robbery!"

"I don't care if it was a triple robbery," Butch said. "We've got to find him. We've got to get that nickel back before he uses it to . . ."

"But he already has!" I broke in excitedly. Because suddenly, I'd remembered something—Kevin Fisher in the library, Kevin almost dropping his soccer ball, Kevin asking the librarian if she was sure a notice wouldn't be sent home, the librarian saying that it wouldn't because he'd already paid.

"Butch!" I exclaimed. "Your nickel's in the library!"

And before anyone could say anything, I grabbed

P.J. by the arm—me dragging her for a change!—and pulled her out the office door, leaving the principal and Monica behind.

Butch, still gripping his bank, was right beside us.

We raced down the hall, past the auditorium, and out the front door. The lights in the library were still on. We dashed across the street and up the steps.

The librarian looked up, startled, as we burst through the door. She was counting coins from the change drawer and rolling them up into neat paper tubes.

"Nickels!" Butch cried, racing to the desk. "We've got to see the nickels."

Before the poor woman could say a word, he'd taken a neatly wrapped roll of nickels and torn the paper open.

"Now, just a minute!" the librarian objected as Butch spread the coins out on the desk.

"It's all right," P.J. said. "We can explain. You see there's this valuable . . ."

"There!" Butch interrupted. "There it is!" He reached out and plucked a shiny nickel from the pile.

I leaned forward.

"See!" Butch said. "Three legs! Boy, I didn't think I'd ever have this in my hands again." He looked sheepishly at P.J. "I guess you win," he said.

To my surprise, P.J. didn't leap up on the desk and crow. Instead, she glanced at the clock on the wall. "You'd better hurry," she said. "Your dad's going to be home in twenty minutes."

"Twenty minutes!" Butch looked at the clock and then at the money spread out on the librarian's desk.

"Don't worry, we'll take care of this," P.J. said.

"I'll say you will," the librarian sputtered. "I want to know the meaning of this. I want to know . . ."

"OK," Butch said, paying no attention to the fuss the librarian was making. "And . . . uh . . ." He ducked his head so he wouldn't have to look P.J. in the eye. "Thanks," he muttered quickly, and dashed out into the night.

P.J. was strangely quiet.

"What's wrong?" I said as a short time later we headed through the crowd of parents leaving the auditorium at Park School.

It seemed to me that things couldn't be more right. We'd explained everything to the librarian, and we'd stopped by to tell Mr. McMurphy, who was having a heart-to-heart talk with Monica in his mouse-filled office, what had happened.

We'd gotten an invitation from him for all three of us—Butch, P.J., and me—to go to the Mickey Mouse collectors' show. "I don't think that bank is in good enough condition to be worth a thousand dollars," he'd said. "But it might be worth several hundred."

That, plus solving the case—even though it had been in a backward sort of way—winning the bet, and having Butch Bigelow actually thank us seemed good enough to me.

"I don't know," P.J. said with a shrug. She blew a strand of straggly blond hair out of her eyes. "I guess I'm going to miss him, that's all."

"Who?" I said.

"Butch," P.J. replied. "I mean, if he keeps his part of the bargain and doesn't bug us anymore . . ." She let her voice trail off.

"You mean you *want* him to pick on us?" I exclaimed. "You want him to pull dirty tricks like sending that little boy with the missing—"

I was going to say "cookie jar" when suddenly I remembered that Butch *hadn't* sent the boy to us—at least not the second time. There really *was* a Mickey Mouse cookie jar missing!

And sheets. How could I have forgotten about my brother Victor's Mickey Mouse sheets?

"P.J.!" I exclaimed. "This case isn't over. We still don't know what happened to . . ."

But just then, I heard my mother's voice. "Stacy Jones," she called. We'd stopped just outside the auditorium door. I'd forgotten that we weren't supposed to be here. That I was supposed to be home safe in bed. "Come here," my mother called. "You too, P.J. Clover."

"Uh oh," I muttered, forgetting for the moment about the sheets and the cookie jar. "Now we're in—"

But before I could say "trouble," P.J. grabbed my arm. "Stacy!" she said. "Look!" She pointed to the refreshment table just inside the auditorium door.

Covering it was the brightly patterned cloth I'd seen earlier in the evening. Now that I was closer, I could see the pictures on it. Pictures of a jaunty, big-eared . . . "Victor's Mickey Mouse sheets!" I exclaimed.

"And I'll bet that's the cookie jar," P.J. said, pointing to an oversize ceramic Mickey perched at one end of the table.

Decorations for the new principal. Of course!

"Do you like them?" my mother asked, forgetting

for the moment to be angry. "Mr. McMurphy did. Butch Bigelow was impressed too."

"Butch!" P.J.'s ears perked up. "Was he here?"

"Just for a second," my mother replied. "He was in a big hurry. He said you two would probably be along soon. He said you'd explain everything." She eyed me narrowly. "And *that* is going to take some doing," she warned. "He also asked me to give you this."

She reached into her pocket and pulled out a piece of paper. P.J. grabbed it eagerly. It was covered with Butch's familiar handwriting. It said:

You did OK... this time.
But I'll bet you couldn't
solve a real crime!

"Real crime!" P.J. exclaimed. "Couldn't solve . . ."

She turned to me. The light was back in her eyes. Mickey was beaming from her chest. "Well, he's got another think coming," she declared. "We'll show him. We'll *really* show him. Next time!"

ABOUT THE AUTHOR

Susan Meyers based P.J. Clover's detective agency on a crime-solving business that her daughter started when she was about P.J.'s age. Her inspiration for *The Case of the Missing Mouse* came from a junior high school principal who is a collector of Mickey Mouse memorabilia.

The West Coast editor of *Enter* magazine, Ms. Meyers lives in San Francisco, California. She has written several other books for children, including P.J. CLOVER PRIVATE EYE: #1 The Case of the Stolen Laundry and P.J. CLOVER PRIVATE EYE: *#3 The Case of the Borrowed Baby*.

ABOUT THE ILLUSTRATOR

Gioia Fiammenghi, a native of New York City, now lives in Monte Carlo. The mother of three sons, she speaks four langauges fluently and has traveled widely.

Educated at Parson's School of Design in New York and Europe, Ms. Fiammenghi has illustrated more than seventy books for children.